Christmas by the Sea

A Haunting by the Sea Mystery

by

Kathi Daley

This book is a work of fiction. Names, characters, places, and incidents either are products of the author's imagination or are used fictitiously. Any resemblance to actual events or locales or persons, living or dead, is entirely coincidental.

Version 1.0

Haunting by the Sea

Homecoming by the Sea
Secrets by the Sea
Missing by the Sea
Betrayal by the Sea
Thanksgiving by the Sea
Christmas by the Sea

Chapter 1

The fire danced and warmed the room as fluffy flakes of snow drifted effortlessly on drafts of air outside my window. The snow didn't have a plan. It didn't have a destination. It simply allowed itself to go where the wind took it without ever stopping to worry or even to have an opinion about it. Sometimes when life became too much, I'd focus on the simplicity of the life of a snowflake.

"Meow."

I turned away from the window to find my cat, Shadow, staring at me.

"Sorry. I know you are looking for dinner, but I guess I floated away for a moment."

He jumped off the bed and wandered to the closed door. Mom was downstairs in the kitchen, and whatever she was cooking smelled wonderful. It would only be the two of us this evening, along with Shadow and the dogs, of course. My roommate and best friend, Mackenzie Reynolds, was visiting her boyfriend, Ty Matthews, for the weekend, and my *sort of maybe someday* boyfriend, Trevor Johnson, worked at the restaurant he owned on Saturdays.

It had been a long time since Mom and I had spent Christmas together in the house by the sea. Ten years to be exact. We'd lived here for two years while in witness protection, but once their own family members had eliminated the men who were after me, we'd returned to New York where we'd lived before the disruption to our lives. I supposed in a life made up of twenty-seven Christmases to date, two wouldn't seem like a significant number, but the two spent in tiny Cutter's Cove with Mac, Trevor, Mom, and my dog, Tucker, were the best two of my life.

Until now. Now I had Christmas with Mac, Trevor, Mom, and Tucker to look forward to, but this Christmas we'd be adding Sunny, the newest four-legged addition to the family, Shadow, my cat and confidant, Mac's boyfriend, Ty, and my previous handler and current friend, Donovan, who I really should call and check in with. About two months ago, I'd received a threatening text which hadn't really led to anything, but I knew it was in my own best interest to stay on top of things, so *things* didn't wind up on top of me.

Picking up the burner cell he'd given me to use, I dialed his private number. Until I'd received that threatening text from an unknown source, I'd thought I was done with Mario and Clay Bonatello, the brothers who had forced me into witness protection when I was a teenager. The text included a photo of the brothers and a message that said: *She who spills the blood must pay the price.* Before their own family murdered them, Mario and Clay had worked for them.

After I witnessed them killing a man in cold blood, they had set out to eliminate the only witness to their crime. I'd been placed in witness protection and had thought myself safe until they found out where I was living and sent someone to kill me. Eventually, my mom and I got a message from Donovan, which assured me that the boss of the Bonatello family had decided he was tired of cleaning up the brothers' messes, so they'd been eliminated, and suddenly, after two years in hiding, Mom and I were free to return to our home in New York. I hadn't been back to Cutter's Cove until this past spring when I returned to help solve the murder of a friend. When I first notified Donovan about the text, he had no idea who had sent it or why, but he had promised to keep an ear to the ground. He also took my cell and gave me a burner to use.

Since then, Donovan had confirmed that the man we thought might be behind the threat was Clay's son, Vito Bonatello, who, in a bid for control of the family, was suspected of being responsible for the deaths of five high-ranking family members. He'd been sure Vito was behind the text to me, but then he found out that the police had detained Vito on another charge when the text was sent, so it couldn't have been him. We suspected he may have had help sending the message, but when Donovan spoke to Vito, he swore he had bigger fish to fry than messing around with childish texts. Nothing more came from the message, so it looked as if the whole thing was just a prank.

"Amanda. How are you?" Donovan asked after answering my call.

"I'm fine. I was just sitting here thinking about the fact that we hadn't spoken for a few weeks and decided to check in. Do you have any news?"

"I do. In fact, I was going to call you as soon as I had a chance to look into things a bit."

"Bad news?"

"Perhaps." He cleared his throat. "I received another text from the same blocked number on the cell phone I took from you. My tech guys are trying to backtrack it to determine where the text originated, which is why I was waiting to call. So far, they haven't had any luck."

"Should I be worried?"

"I think you should be cautious," Donovan answered. "We've discussed the fact that it appears that whoever is sending the texts believes you're in New York. And while that may still be true, the new text feels more like a message or a clue than a generalized threat. It somehow feels specific."

Okay, that had me frowning. "What do you mean specifically? What does the text say?"

"The second text is actually a two-part text. The first part is a threat about spilling the blood and paying the price, very similar to the first text you received a couple of months ago. That was followed by a second part that reads: *The shuttered window won't hide the truth.*"

"What does that mean?"

"I don't know," Donovan admitted. "But after I read the text, it occurred to me that when I visited at Thanksgiving, I'd noticed that you have wooden shutters on the exterior of your home. Of course, a lot of people have wooden shutters, and the threat is vague, but since there has been a new text, I feel like you should keep your eyes open."

I wanted to launch into a tirade about never being free of the men who had already taken so much from me, but I knew Donovan was doing the best that he could, so I kept my complaints to myself. "Okay. Thanks for the heads up."

"If we're able to locate the source of the texts, or if we get any more information about the context of the texts, I will definitely let you know."

"I appreciate that. I'm looking forward to you being with us for Christmas."

"Me too. I've been chatting with your mother, and she's been describing the town's decorations. It sounds just like the Christmases I used to have as a child."

"Didn't you grow up in New York?" I asked.

"No, I actually grew up in Iowa, where small-town America is at its best."

"That sounds nice. I don't think I've ever been to Iowa. Do you visit often?"

"I haven't been back in years."

Based on the way he said it, I suspected there was a story there, but I didn't ask. "I guess I should go. I think Mom has dinner ready. Before I hang up, I've been wondering and would like to know if Donovan is your first name or last name."

"Last. My name is Sam Donovan. When I was a kid, everyone called me Sammy, but since I joined the agency, everyone has called me Donovan. I'll see you next week if I don't talk to you before then."

"Yes. I'll see you then." I clicked off my phone and held it to my chest. I got up from the desk chair where I'd been sitting and crossed to the window. On more than one occasion, Donovan had assured me that I probably wasn't in any sort of immediate danger since it appeared the person sending the texts thought I was still in New York. But shuttered windows? That sounded like something more. Since we lived so close to the sea, when we'd remodeled the first time, Mom had installed heavy wooden shutters on the outside of each window that were usually left open but could be closed if a storm blew in. I'd left them up when I'd bought the house, but so far, I hadn't had a reason to close them. Still, anyone viewing the house from the outside would notice they were there.

I took a deep breath and headed toward the bedroom door. I needed to put on my game face so I wouldn't worry Mom. I knew she'd taken the threat in the first text I'd received seriously.

"There you are." Mom wiped her hands on her cheery Christmas apron when I entered the kitchen. "I wondered where you'd gone off to."

"I was upstairs watching it snow." I picked up a Christmas card addressed to Amanda Parker of Parker Photography. I supposed it might be from one of the few people who actually knew about my new sideline.

"Is something on your mind?"

I shrugged, tossed the card back on the table, crossed the room, and then sat down at the counter that separated the cooking area from the kitchen's small dining area. I didn't intend to worry Mom with news of the text, but she was never going to let it go if I didn't come up with something to share. "I won't say that anything is really wrong, but I will admit that I've been feeling unsettled lately."

"Any particular reason why?"

"I don't know. Nothing is really wrong, it's just that Mac and Ty seem to be moving their relationship forward, and while I am happy for them, I wonder what that will do to what I have with Mac. I've so enjoyed having her as a roommate, and I wonder how it will be living alone in this big old house if she decides to move in with him. It was the two of us living here before, and now it's Mac and me, and I'm just not sure about rambling around here on my own."

Mom took the lid off the pan of spaghetti sauce she'd left simmering on the stove and gave it a good stir. She replaced the lid and then opened the oven to check whatever she was baking. She eventually moved toward the brick fireplace, which was in the center of the room and stood in front of it. "Is that it?" Based on the look on her face, I was pretty sure she didn't believe that was it.

"Well, no," I admitted. "Not really. I guess I'm in a state of flux over my relationship with Trevor as well. I really, really care about him, and while he has been very patient and has allowed me to set the pace, I know he would like to move our relationship to the next level. I suppose there is a part of me that wants that as well, but I'm scared."

"Scared of what?" Mom asked as she returned to the stove.

"Scared of what will happen to our friendship if our romance doesn't work out."

Mom took out a large pot and filled it with water. "I guess I can understand that. Trevor has been in your life for a long time. He fills a void that I'm not sure anyone else would be able to. I suppose it must have occurred to you that what you have now is perfect, and it would be crazy to risk it. Maybe the fact that you have such a perfect friendship might lend itself to the conclusion that you might find that same level of perfection as a couple. I wonder if it might be worth the risk to find out, assuming, of course, there is chemistry between you."

Oh, there was chemistry. Steamy hot chemistry that I was actually amazed hadn't started a fire at some point. I got up and walked over to the cupboard where our glassware was kept. I took out a wine glass and then asked Mom if she would like a glass of wine as well. She nodded that she would. If I was going to have a conversation with my mom about the intimate thoughts I'd been having about Trevor, I was going to need wine.

"Yes, I can say without a doubt that there is chemistry between Trevor and me." I took a bottle of wine from the rack and opened it. "If I really stop to think about it, I have to admit there has always been chemistry between us. Of course, when I lived here as a teenager, I was even less ready for an intimate relationship than I am now." I poured wine into both glasses.

"Did something happen to cause this angst at this point?" Mom wondered.

"Not really. When I first came back to Cutter's Cove, I was still in a relationship with Ethan, which put a natural brake on whatever feelings Trevor and I might have had for each other. By the time I broke things off with Ethan, I guess Trevor and I had both settled back into a friendship, which felt safe and comfortable. But things seem to be evolving naturally, and I'm not sure safe and comfortable is enough for either of us. I'm terrified of moving our relationship out of the friend zone for fear that we'll lose what we have, but I'm also afraid that if I refuse to move our relationship forward, I'll lose him anyway."

Mom slipped a reindeer oven mitt onto one hand. She opened the oven and slid out a tray of bread. "Life is about change. It's about evolving and becoming whatever it is we are meant to be with whomever we're meant to be with. I'm not saying you should jump into anything. I know how much Trevor means to you, and I can see how much you mean to him. But I do think it might be time to open a door that will allow you to at least explore the feelings you seem to share."

I got up, walked around the counter, and gave Mom a hug. "Thanks, Mom."

"Any time."

I took my wine and crossed to the large glass doors that looked out at the sea. It was a dark and blustery day, and I found myself hoping for a lot of snow over the next few days. Snow for Christmas was certainly not a given in the small town on the Oregon coast where I lived, but it was possible, and there had been a few white Christmases in the past.

"Did I tell you about the photography contest my friend from the gallery told me about?" Mom asked.

"Photography contest?" When I'd lived in New York, I'd worked as a graphic designer, but since I'd moved back to Cutter's Cove, I'd refocused my energy into building a photography business, selling stock photos as well as exhibiting some of my better pieces in my mom's gallery back in the Big Apple.

"It's being sponsored by *Backroads Travel.* The contest is geared toward Christmas in small-town

America. Anyone who wishes to submit is welcome to do so. They are looking for a collage of images that showcase a good old fashion Christmas in small towns across the country. I'm afraid you'd only have until the end of the day on Thursday to submit. I would have mentioned it earlier, but I actually just heard about the contest at dinner last night. I know you don't really care about the prize money, but the winning photographer is going to be a featured artist in an upcoming issue of the magazine. I thought that might help you to get the word out about your new venture."

"I'm very interested. Five days isn't a lot of time, but if I get started tomorrow, I'm sure I can come up with something special. The town is already decked out, and it looks like we are going to have enough snow to really set the mood. That'll help. Santa's Village is open, the Christmas Carnival will be up by mid-week, and there are quite a few boats decked out with lights in the marina. Trevor is off tomorrow and Monday, so we had plans to hang out, but I'm sure he'll help me with the project."

"Great. Hang on, and I'll text you the website where you can sign up. It has other information about the size and theme of the entries, as well."

Mom picked up her phone, found the information, and forwarded it to me.

"I'm planning to attend the volunteer meeting for the Christmas Carnival tomorrow," Mom said. "I know I no longer live in Cutter's Cove and therefore am not obligated to volunteer, but I ran into Winnifred Long at the market today, and she told me they are seriously short of help this year."

"Trevor and I volunteered to help out at the Santa House. We have shifts next weekend."

"Are you going to be an elf to Trevor's Santa like you were back in high school?"

"I am," I answered. "I spoke to the volunteer coordinator, and we agreed on a much less revealing costume this time around. If it turns help they need additional help on the weekend, let me know. I'm not going to attend the meeting tomorrow since I want to get started on the photography contest, but I am willing to help if I can."

"I'll let them know. Dinner is ready. Grab the salad from the refrigerator. I thought we'd sit at the little table in the bay window and watch it snow."

"It's dark," I pointed out.

"I know, but the snow looks pretty reflecting off the colorful Christmas lights Trevor strung along the railing and around the windows."

I glanced out the window at the festively decorated deck. In the summer, we'd sit out on the deck and look at the sea. We had the best view from our little corner of the cove. But tonight, with the early darkness of winter, the snow and the lights seemed just about perfect.

Chapter 2

"I think we need to hike up the mountain a bit so we can get a better angle on the families hiking through the trees looking for the perfect specimen to brighten their holiday," I said to Trevor the following day. We were at Dooley's Farm to take photos for my project. Farmer Dooley sold Christmas trees you picked out and cut yourself in the winter, pumpkins you picked from the vine in the fall, and fresh fruit in the spring and summer.

"There's a little path that runs along the perimeter of the cutting area. Maybe we should use that to climb up and then figure out where to set up the camera," Trevor suggested.

"That's a good idea." I called Sunny and Tucker, who'd come along with us on our pilgrimage for the perfect photo. I figured they would enjoy a day out, plus I planned to use them as models at some point during the day. I'd learned you could never go wrong by adding a dog or two to the mix.

"When we finish here, we should stop off at the farm's store for hot cocoa," I suggested. "Farmer Dooley has a special recipe that's to die for."

"They add vanilla ice cream to the mix," Trevor informed me. "When it melts you can stir into the milk and chocolate mixture, making everything thick and creamy." I paused when we were halfway up the hill where the Christmas trees grew. "There." I pointed. "There's a flat spot where we can set up, and there aren't a lot of trees in the way. The light is behind us, and quite a few families are searching for the perfect tree just below us. We should be able to get some excellent shots."

Once Trevor and I got set up, I attached the camera to the tripod and then focused the lens. The little girl with blond hair and a red knit cap chasing her brother with blond hair and a green cap made fun subjects. There was a family of five drinking hot cocoa, and a short woman with dark hair, standing alone looking toward the mountain. I paused on her face, which seemed familiar, but then, deciding I didn't know her, continued to scan the crowd, snapping as many photos as I could. Once I got back to the house, I'd sort through them looking for anything that might be special enough to use.

"Where do you want to go next?" Trevor asked after I'd snapped at least a hundred photos.

"Santa's Village and then the ice skating rink in the park. I'd like to photograph the skaters as the sky darkens at dusk. After that, we can walk around town and grab photos of the Christmas windows and people shopping, and then maybe we can have dinner. They do that big lighting display and live nativity on the wharf, so maybe we can eat there."

“Sounds good. It’s too bad Mac and Ty are in Portland this weekend. They’re missing out.”

I shrugged. “They are, but I am enjoying just the two of us spending time together. In fact, I thought that maybe when we’re done for the day, we could head over to your place on the beach and build a fire in your pit. We can share a bottle of wine and maybe cuddle up in your two-person lounge chair and watch the waves roll onto the snow-covered beach.”

That had Trevor grinning from ear to ear. I’d thought about my talk with my mom last night, and I’d pretty much decided that I’d talk to Trevor about our relationship tonight. Of course, if I was honest with myself, it wasn’t talking that was on my mind.

“Check out that little boy with the red jacket over to the right.” I focused my camera in for the shot. The boy was probably five or six. He was dragging a red sled up the hill, but the weight of the thing seemed to be almost more than he could handle. I’d noticed him stopping every ten yards or so, and when he did, the golden retriever puppy that was with him, would jump on him and lick his face, which would cause him to fall back in the snow laughing. Each time he fell, he’d let go of the sled which would slide back down the mountain to about the same place where he’d started.

“He’s never going to make it to the top of the hill that way,” Trevor said.

I snapped shot after shot. “To be honest, I don’t think he cares. He’s obviously having the time of this life playing with that puppy.”

“I wonder where his parents are.”

Good question. I used my telephoto lens to scan the surrounding area. “There,” I said, pointing. “They aren’t too far away, just behind that grove of trees.”

I scanned back over to the boy who had gotten himself up and had started up the hill once again. I watched as the man I assumed was his father called for him. He called back, sat down on his sled, and slid toward the clearing where the man and woman I thought were his parents were waiting. Once he reached the young couple, the man lifted the boy onto his shoulders, the woman took possession of the sled, and they began to walk toward the parking area.

“What about the puppy?” I wondered.

I continued to watch, but the puppy wasn’t with them.

“Maybe the puppy doesn’t belong to the boy,” Trevor said. “Maybe they just ran into each other and stopped to play.”

I used my camera to scan the area. “Okay, then where are the puppy’s humans. He couldn’t have been more than four months old.”

Trevor turned his head slowly. I could see that he was looking for the little dog the same as me. “Maybe we should head over to where we saw the puppy and boy playing, and see if we can find him.”

I picked up my tripod. “Let’s go.”

When we arrived at the spot where I’d seen the boy and the puppy playing, I called for him. When he didn’t come, I instructed Tucker to find him. Sunny was not as skilled at finding things as Tucker was, but she ran along behind him anyway.

“I hope he isn’t lost,” I said as worry set in.

"We'll find him," Trevor assured me. "It looks like there are puppy size prints that go off in that direction." He pointed. "Let's follow them."

I could hear Tucker and Sunny rustling around in the shrubs in front of us. They seemed to be trying to pick up the scent. After a few minutes, Tucker came running back toward us, with Sunny on his heels. He had something in his mouth. I told him to drop it when he arrived at the spot where I was standing.

"It's a shoe," Trevor said.

I looked at Tucker. I showed him the shoe. "Find the other one," I commanded.

He turned and started back the way he'd just come. Somehow, I knew even before Tucker showed me what he'd found, that the something he wanted to show me, would not only be the other shoe but the *someone* who'd been wearing it.

Chapter 3

"And you didn't notice anyone else in the area?" Officer Woody Baker asked me after I'd called him.

"No," I answered. "Trevor and I are here taking photos for a contest I've entered. We noticed a young boy playing with a puppy who was so cute. After a while, a man who I assume was the boy's father, called to the boy, and he went toward the parking area with his parents. Trevor and I didn't see the puppy, so we went to look for him and found the body." I looked toward the remains of the female victim who was covered with a layer of snow. She was dressed in denim jeans, a bright red sweater, and red high-heeled pumps. Or at least one red pump. "Do you know who she is?"

"Not offhand. What I do know is those shoes are totally impractical for a hike up this mountain, and she would have frozen to death without a jacket. The sweater is pretty but thin. More for indoor wear."

"I agree. It looks to me as if she was dumped here." I looked around the area. It had snowed overnight, so any tracks that might have been left would have been snowed over.

"It wouldn't have been easy to hike up the mountain carrying a body," Woody pointed out.

"True. But there is that old jeep trail that climbs up the mountain from the backside. It would be tough to navigate with the snow but not impossible with a four-wheel-drive. If a four-wheel-drive did access the mountain from the top, it would be easy enough to just toss the body and let it roll to where it had landed."

Woody scanned the area. "I guess it could have happened that way. I'll be sure to check the jeep trail for tire tracks or any other evidence that someone accessed it recently. It snowed overnight, which will make things tough, but there might be something to find." He looked around. "You said you were with Trevor. Where is he?"

"He took Tucker and Sunny and is looking for the puppy. The poor little guy seemed to be lost, and we wanted to find him before we leave. I agreed to wait with the body until you arrived."

"I don't suppose your ghost friend who helps you with these sorts of things is around."

I knew he was referring to Alyson, my ghostly counterpart. "No. She hasn't shown up. I'll try to contact her. Sometimes she just pops in, and sometimes it takes a while. Do you need me to stay here? If not, I think I'll join Trevor in his search for the puppy."

"I'll need to process the area. It will take a while. I, of course, want to know if you make contact with the ghost of the victim or if your ghost sidekick shows up."

"I'll let you know," I promised. "In fact, feel free to call or text me at any time. I can meet you at your office, or wherever you want."

He nodded. "Okay. It looks like the units I called for backup are here. I'll call you later, and we can compare notes."

I texted Trevor and asked him where he was. He texted me his GPS location, and I headed in that direction.

"Any luck?" I asked.

"Not yet. The puppy seems to have continued up the mountain after he left the boy. Tucker seems to have picked up the trail, so I'm just following him."

"Okay. Let's continue." I motioned for Tucker to continue his search for the puppy.

It took us another hour of searching since the puppy seemed to have zig-zagged rather than walking in a straight line, but we eventually found an entrance to a shallow cave where it looked like the puppy had been living. I didn't see any other dogs or people in the area, so I bribed the puppy to follow us by offering small pieces of the granola bar I had in my pocket. Once he came all the way out of his hiding place, Trevor picked him up, and we headed down the mountain to the lot where we'd left Trevor's truck.

"Okay, so what should we do now?" Trevor asked once we had all three dogs loaded into the backseat.

"Let's take the dogs home. I can call animal control and see if anyone has reported a missing puppy. If not, I'll get him settled in my room. I want to see if I can contact Alyson. I called for her when we first found the body, but she didn't appear."

"And you didn't see a ghost that might have been associated with the body?" Trevor asked.

"No, I didn't see a ghost. Either the woman moved on right away, and there isn't a ghost to find, or she was scared and hiding. It's also possible the ghost is trapped at the location where she died. It seems unlikely that the woman died up here on this mountain."

"Why don't you think she died here?" Trevor asked.

"She was dressed totally wrong for a trek up the mountain. I suspect she died elsewhere and was dumped where we found her."

"It would take a lot of effort to carry another person up the mountain through the snow," Trevor pointed out.

"That's what Woody said, but we discussed the idea that someone could have brought her up on the old jeep trail that climbs up the mountain from the backside and then tossed the body and let it roll to where we found it."

"It did look as if she had been rolled in the snow, and I suppose someone might have brought the body up here from the backside, but it seems there are easier and less public places to dump a body," Trevor pointed out.

"I don't disagree. I guess we won't know anything for sure until the medical examiner has a chance to take a look."

When we arrived at the house, Trevor headed into the kitchen to make a pot of coffee, and I headed upstairs to get the puppy settled and to call animal control to see if anyone had reported a puppy missing. No one had. I set him up with a bed, food and water, and toys in the bathroom. I wasn't sure if he was housebroken, and I didn't want to test his bladder control on the hardwood floors, so I set up a child gate to keep him confined. Sunny was fascinated with him and laid down on the other side of the gate. Both dogs fell asleep before I even left the room.

Once I got the puppy settled, I called for Alyson once again, but she didn't reply. Deciding to leave the dogs to their nap, I headed back downstairs, where Trevor greeted me with a mug of hot coffee.

"Your mom isn't here?" he asked.

"I guess she must still be at the Christmas Carnival meeting."

"And still no word from Alyson?"

I shook my head.

"I've tried not to be overly nosy about Alyson and the relationship you share, but how exactly does it work? Where does she go when she isn't here, and how are you able to contact her when you need her?"

I let out a short breath. "Honestly, I'm not sure I totally understand myself, but she seems to be a detachable part of me. I think when she isn't needed to help me with whichever ghost I'm meant to help, she exists as part of me on the inside. Then when a ghost appears, poof, she appears as well."

"So, maybe she isn't responding because there's no ghost in need of help," Trevor suggested.

"Maybe. Although she did appear at the hospital when I was trying to help the social worker who'd been shot, and there was no ghost then either."

"True, but in that situation, your help was needed. Hers was as well. Maybe in this instance, neither of you are destined to be part of whatever is going on."

I shrugged. "Maybe. There isn't a ghost at this point, so even if Alyson did show up, there wouldn't be anything for her to do. And Woody hasn't asked for our help, so she may be waiting until she is needed."

"So, what do you want to do now?" he asked.

I glanced out the window at the gently falling snow. "I guess we should continue with our plans. If a ghost appears, or Woody calls and asks for our help, we'll drop everything and do what we can. In the meantime, let's visit Santa and then head to the ice skating rink."

"Are you bringing your skates?" Trevor asked.

"Sure. Why not? I wouldn't mind taking a spin or two around the rink."

"And the dogs?"

"They're all sleeping upstairs. The puppy is in the bathroom. I have a child gate across the entrance. I hate to leave him locked up, but I don't know if he's housebroken, and I don't want puppy piddle to ruin the hardwood floor."

"You have a big bathroom. I'm sure he'll be fine. If you want, we can go to the village and take your photos, and then stop back by here and check on the dogs before heading to the skating rink."

I picked up my camera bag. "That sounds like a good plan. We can take them out when we get back. If the puppy didn't piddle in the bathroom, maybe I'll let him have the run of the house. He is old enough to have been housebroken. I just don't know if anyone did it."

Chapter 4

Santa's Village had been set up at the far end of the park and included a structure made to look like a gingerbread house, where children could sit on Santa's lap, take a photo, and get a candy cane. There was also a section of the building set up to sell ornaments, copies of the photos, candy, and other holiday fare. Based on the long line leading up to the place, it seemed as if the entire town had shown up to tell their wishes to the jolly bearded man in red.

"My favorite part of Santa's Village is actually the displays set up outside the house," Trevor said.

I lifted my camera and began to capture images of happy kids and enchanting decorations. "I totally agree. The mechanical penguins on the frozen lake, the polar bears sliding down the icy mountain, and the raccoons decorating the trees in the forest are all fantastic. I think I'm going to get some really good shots. Once I get enough out here, we'll head inside."

"Are you going to set up the tripod?"

"No," I answered. "I'm just going to take a bunch of photos from random angles and see what I end up with." I had to admit the festive atmosphere had me smiling. There were happy children, carols playing over the loudspeaker, and mechanical decorations displayed around hundreds of decorated trees.

I made my rounds and was about to head inside and get photos of children on Santa's lap while adults shopped for special treats or a handcrafted ornament when my phone buzzed. I looked at the caller ID. It was Woody. I hit answer.

"Hey, Woody, did you ID our victim?"

"Holly Quinn. Holly is twenty-four years old and works part-time at the Bayside Grill. She did a volunteer shift at Santa's Village yesterday with Owen Anderson, the man who played Santa to her elf. According to Mr. Anderson, Holly completed her shift and then changed into her street clothes. She told Owen that she had a date at The Rusty Nail, which is just across the park from the Santa House. Owen noticed that she had on red heels, so he offered to drop her off. He said he dropped her in front of the bar and continued on."

"Do we know who the date was with?"

"The man she met is a local real estate agent named Christopher Cartwright. Most people call him Chris. I spoke to Mr. Cartwright, and he said that Holly met him at the bar, and the pair shared a couple of drinks. He'd made plans for them to have dinner, but then he got a call from his office about a break-in at one of the properties he had listed, so he had to leave. I've been able to verify that there was a break-in at a house being sold by Cartwright, so his alibi seems legit."

"What did Holly do after Cartwright left?"

"It sounds like she finished her drink and then left. No one I've spoken to seems to know where she went after she left the bar."

"She couldn't have gone far with the shoes she had on."

"I agree. Her shoes were not made for walking, especially not in the snow."

"So, it sounds like the first task is going to be to try to determine where Holly went after she left the bar."

"That is the challenge at this point. So far, no one I've spoken to claims to have seen her. I did speak to one of the cocktail waitresses who worked at The Rusty Nail that evening. She said she ran into Holly in the ladies' room shortly before she left. Holly told her that she wasn't feeling well and was going to call one of her roommates for a ride home. I spoke to all four of Holly's roommates, and they all claim that she never called. They also claim that she never came home. If I had to bet, I'd say she ran into someone who offered her a ride, and that someone is most likely the person who killed her."

"Do you know the cause of death?"

"Not yet. The medical examiner is working on it. Holly doesn't appear to have any visible injuries other than bruising on her cheek, so we can eliminate obvious causes such as shooting, stabbing, and blunt force trauma. I'm afraid this might be a tough one to solve. A victim who was able to tell us what happened would really help. I don't suppose that a ghost might have shown up?"

"No. I'm sorry. I can go back to the spot where the body was found and take another look around, but I didn't sense anyone when I was there."

"And Alyson?"

"Seems to be unavailable at the moment."

"If it isn't too much trouble, I'd love it if you would meet me at the house Holly was living in. The roommates all claim that she never called for a ride and never came home, but the easiest explanation is that she did go home, and one of her roommates killed her and then dumped her body. I figure if she died in that house, then maybe her spirit is still there."

I glanced at the Santa House. It would be there tomorrow, and this seemed important. "I can do that. Trevor and I are in town. Just give me the address."

After I filled Trevor in, we stopped by my house, checked on the dogs, confirmed there were no puppy piddles to find, and let them out to run. I knew my mom would be home soon, so I texted her about the puppy, and she agreed to let him out when she got home. Since he had just peed, I decided it was probably safe to give him the run of the house with the other dogs.

Trevor and I then headed to the address Woody had given me. When we arrived, Woody's car was already in the drive. Trevor and I joined him.

"Is anyone here?" I asked.

"No. The roommates are all at work. I told them I was coming by to look through Holly's things and have permission to enter. I didn't explain that I was bringing a ghost whisperer along, but I suppose that's something they don't need to know."

"Okay. Let's head inside."

Once we entered the house, I paused and looked around. The place was a total mess. There was garbage on the floor, dishes in the sink as well as on every available countertop, and laundry was piled almost to the ceiling in the laundry room. What did these guys think was going to happen? The housework elves would come by at night if they just left everything where it landed. I really didn't see how anyone could live like this.

"Anything?" Woody asked after I had walked around for a moment.

"No. Not yet. It might be better if I look around alone. Maybe you and Trevor can wait here, and I'll take a walk around and see if anyone shows up."

"Fine with me," Woody agreed.

I decided to start upstairs. If the woman we'd found in the woods had been killed in this house and her ghost was indeed trapped here, I figured she would be more likely to make herself known if there weren't a lot of people around.

"Holly," I said as I walked through the house. "My name is Amanda. If you're here and can hear me, I'm here to help you."

I walked slowly through the structure, entering each room as I continued to speak. The house was actually nice beneath the filth. It had five bedrooms, four baths, a large living room, a den, a country kitchen, and a formal dining area. The bedroom that I decided must have belonged to Holly was clean and organized, as was the adjoining bath, but the rest of the house was a pigpen. It looked as if the tenants of the other four bedrooms were all male. I had to wonder how Holly had come to live with them.

After I had entered and searched every room, I headed back to where Trevor and Woody were waiting. “I’m sorry,” I said. “Holly’s ghost isn’t here. To be honest, I’m not picking up on any sort of vibe that would indicate violence has occurred on the property. Is there anything else we can help you with?”

“No. Thank you for taking the time to look around.”

“If you change your mind and decide you do have something else we can help with, just call,” I offered.

After Woody left, Trevor and I chatted about it and decided we’d missed our window for the skating pictures and would have to get them tomorrow. We still wanted to eat and maybe grab some photos of the lights in town but decided to stop off at our respective residences to change and clean up a bit before heading to dinner. Of course, once we arrived at my place, Mom was home, and the warmth from the cozy fire, combined with Christmas jazz, a fully decorated room, a bottle of wine, and a cheese and olive tray, had me suggesting that maybe we just stay in this evening. Trevor wanted to change his clothes even if we were staying in, so he headed home, promising to pick up some food on his way back.

“This is so nice.” I laid my head on Mom’s shoulder. Tucker, who was laying on the sofa next to me was snoring softly while the puppy was sleeping in front of the fire with Sunny.

“It really is. I’ve missed this since you went off to college, and we no longer lived together.”

“Me too,” I said. “Were there any puppy accidents when you got home?”

"Not a one, which leads me to wonder why a housebroken puppy would be living alone in the woods. It makes sense that he might have wandered away from home, but if that's true, why isn't someone looking for him?"

"I don't know," I responded, narrowing my gaze. "I really thought someone would have called the shelter by now."

"He's an adorable puppy and so well behaved. I can't believe that someone would have just dumped him."

"Unfortunately, it does happen, but he looks healthy and well-fed, so maybe we'll get a call tomorrow."

"Have your plans for tomorrow changed?" Mom asked.

"No. Not unless a ghost shows up. So far, I don't feel like I have a role in this investigation."

"You did find the body," she pointed out.

"That's true."

"It is such a shame," she said in a soft voice. "A real tragedy. The poor girl was younger than you are. She'd barely had a chance to get started on life."

"I know." I gave Mom's hand a squeeze. I could sense that talking about the dead girl was upsetting her, so I changed the subject and asked about the Christmas Carnival meeting.

"It was productive," she shared. "There's still a lot to do and such a short amount of time to get it all done, but I'm confident we will pull it all together in time."

"I remember when we lived here before, and you were the chairwoman, and everything that could go wrong did go wrong," I chucked.

"Don't even say such a thing. The last thing we need is for this year's event to go the way that one did. Talk about a disaster."

"It wasn't all that bad." I tried to sound encouraging. "Yes, there were bad moments, but it all worked out okay."

"You almost died," she reminded me.

"Yes, I guess there was that. But I actually have fond memories of that Christmas. In fact, I think it was one of my favorites."

Tucker lifted his head and looked toward the door. Always the watchdog. "It sounds like Trevor is back. I wonder what he brought to eat. Even though I've been nibbling on the cheese, I'm still starving."

As it turned out, Trevor brought enchiladas and Chile Rellenos from the Mexican place. He picked up sides of refried beans, Mexican rice, and chips and salsa. It was actually the perfect meal for a cold and snowy night. We set everything up buffet style, we each made a plate and ate in front of the fire.

"I ran into Woody while I was in town," Trevor said after we'd all gotten our food.

"Did he have an update?" I asked.

"We were standing in line at the restaurant picking up food, so he didn't want to get into it, but he did say he had new information to share. I mentioned that we planned to have dinner here, and he said he'd call you when he had the chance."

"It'd be nice if he could get the case closed quickly," Mom said. "I'm afraid that given the ambiguity of the cause of death, there are going to be a lot of rumors circulating once word gets out."

Trevor got up and served himself another chicken enchilada. Once he took a scoop of rice, he sat back down. “We discussed the fact that it seemed likely, given the location where the body was found, that someone accessed the mountain using a four-wheel-drive vehicle via the old jeep trail and dumped her after she was already dead. We know that Holly had been dropped off at the bar and needed to find a ride home. Woody spoke to the roommates, who all swear she didn’t call them, so we’re assuming she found someone else to give her a ride. What if Holly came up the mountain with whoever offered her a ride? Maybe it was someone she’d been dating, and they planned to see the lights and make out. During this make-out session, Holly became angry for some reason and left the vehicle. Maybe the guy had crossed a line of some sort, and she wanted to make it clear she was having nothing of it.”

“But it was freezing. It seems foolish to wander out into the snow to escape a handsy date,” I pointed out.

“That’s true, but if Holly had been drinking heavily, she may not have even realized how cold it actually was,” Trevor argued.

“Trevor makes a good point,” Mom said. “If this young woman did access the mountain via the jeep trail and had been drinking heavily, it seems believable she might have left the vehicle she voluntarily arrived in and simply froze to death.”

“If that’s what happened, then it seems like whoever just left her there is to blame for what happened,” I pointed out. “I guess we’ll know more once we have the official cause of death.”

“Maybe her cause of death is the news Woody has to share,” Trevor suggested.

After we ate, Mom volunteered to clean up while Trevor and I took the dogs out for a walk. Unlike Holly, we bundled up like we were going for a stroll in the North Pole.

"Are you going to keep the puppy if you don't find his owner?" Trevor asked.

"I guess I will. I'm hesitant to get too attached at this point. He appears to be in good health and well-fed, so it's unlikely he's been on his own for too long. He seems to be a sweetie, and he gets along with Tucker and Sunny."

Trevor took my hand in his while we walked. "Maybe you should give him a name."

"Not yet. I'm going to make a few calls and maybe put up some fliers out at Dooley's Farm and in the neighborhood on the other side of the mountain. If we don't find the owner in a few days, I'll name him. For now, I think calling him puppy is fine."

"Personally, I like Cooper. Coop for short."

"I like Cooper," I agreed. "If I do end up keeping him, I will definitely consider that name. I'll need to check with Mac. I sort of remember her mentioning an ex named Cooper. I wouldn't want to bring up bad memories every time I call the dog."

Trevor twisted his lips. "I thought I knew about all of Mac's boyfriends, and I don't remember a Cooper but maybe. It's a good idea to ask her. Will she be home tomorrow?"

"I think she's coming home tomorrow afternoon."

Trevor stopped walking. We paused to look out over the sea. "So, what are we planning for tomorrow?"

"I thought we'd pick up where we left off with the photos. I need the interior of the Santa House, the ice skating rink, the downtown area after dark, and the big tree in the park. If we have time, I'd like to get some kids sledding and maybe some scenes with families drinking hot cocoa."

"Sounds like a full day."

I nodded. "It will be, but it will be fun as well."

Trevor turned, so we were face to face. He slid his arms around my waist. "I'm really glad we could be together this Christmas."

"I'm happy about that too."

"I've been thinking a lot about that last Christmas we were all together here in Cutter's Cove before you went back to New York. Back then, in that moment, I really thought we'd share all our Christmases together, but we didn't."

"No," I admitted. "We didn't."

"But we're together now."

I reached up and wrapped my arms around his neck. "We are together now. What do you say we make up for all the Christmases we missed and make this the best one we've ever had?"

"I'm on board for that."

I pulled Trevor's head toward mine. When our lips tentatively met, I leaned in to deepen the kiss. I really didn't know what the future had in store for us, but in this moment, on a snowy night overlooking the sea, I knew I was exactly where I was meant to be.

Chapter 5

Woody never called the previous evening, so I supposed he might have gotten tied up with the investigation. I figured I'd get up, grab some coffee and breakfast, and if I still hadn't heard from him, I'd give him a call. Trevor planned to come by at ten, so we could resume our photo gathering. Many of the photos I wanted to capture needed to be taken at dusk or even after dark, but the interior of the Santa House, along with photos of daytime activities such as snowman building and sleigh rides, could be taken at any point in the day.

"I guess the first thing I need to do is take you all out for a quick run," I said to the three dogs who were looking at me with expectation in their eyes. So far, the puppy hadn't had any accidents. I considered that to be a good sign.

I pulled on heavy pants, a thick sweater, and heavy boots. My jacket, hat, and gloves were downstairs, so I headed in that direction. It didn't sound like Mom was up yet, so I left a brief note and headed out the door. I couldn't believe it was still snowing. Not a lot, just flurries, but for some reason, the little frozen flakes drifting through the air made me crazy happy.

I'd spent some time thinking about Alyson last night and decided to try calling her again. In the beginning, when I'd first come back to Cutter's Cove, she'd lived exclusively on the outside, a parallel life of sorts to mine. Once I'd made the commitment to stay in Cutter's Cove rather than returning to New York, she'd begun to integrate with the part of my essence I considered to be me. Initially, she'd show up frequently on the outside, even if it was just to chat, but the longer I stayed in Cutter's Cove, the less frequently she appeared as an external entity.

The fact that she wasn't showing up now even though I'd called for her had me wondering if at some point the reintegration of my two parts would be complete and she would cease to appear as a separate being altogether. Initially, that was what I'd wanted, but now that we'd spent some time working together, it seemed obvious that having a part of myself that could go where I could not was really convenient at times.

"Alyson, if you can hear me, I'd really like to speak to you," I said aloud. "I realize we don't have a ghost to help at the moment, but there has been a death."

I waited, but she didn't show. I tried a few more times and finally decided to give up. I supposed if Trevor and I did move our relationship toward a place where intimate relations would be part of the package, it might be nice not to have to worry about

Alyson popping in and out of my life. Even just talking to Alyson about Trevor felt awkward and weird the few times we'd discussed her obvious crush on him. Maybe it was time for the two of us to become one. I really couldn't imagine how this would work in the future.

I'd just called the dogs so we could turn around and head back to the house when my phone buzzed. It was Woody.

"Hey, Woody."

"I'm sorry I wasn't able to call you last night. Things got sort of crazy, and before I knew it, it was too late to call."

"No problem. Do you have news?"

"Holly had a significant amount of a drug that works as a hallucinogen in her system when she died. The official cause of death is still under investigation, but the medical examiner did say that the drug could be a contributing factor."

"So, are we thinking she took the drugs voluntarily?" I asked.

Woody blew out a breath. "I don't know. She could have died as the result of recreational drug use, or she could have been dosed without knowing about it. She had whiskey in her stomach, but not much else. If she'd been drinking and doing drugs, that could have led to her death. It's also possible that someone slipped the drugs into her drink."

"Maybe she died due to drug use, but she didn't walk up the mountain where I found her in heels," I pointed out. "Someone has to have dumped her there, which in my mind suggests foul play rather than an accident."

"I agree. I'm working from the idea that she was murdered and dumped, but at this point, I don't have a lot to go on. If she was killed, chances are she was killed by whoever she met up with after Cartwright left the bar to check on the break-in."

"Someone must have seen something."

"I agree. I just haven't managed to track down that someone yet."

"You'll figure it out."

"I hope I can catch a break soon. Both her mother and her grandmother are breathing down my neck to find the killer."

"Do they live in town?"

"No. They live in Tennessee."

"And did they know if she had a history of drug abuse?"

"They both insist that while she has been known to smoke a little marijuana, she would never take hard drugs, and therefore she must have been dosed by someone who either intended to kill her or at the very least intended to cause her harm. I'm afraid that if she did simply OD on her own, I may never be able to give these women the closure they're looking for."

"You are in a tough spot," I admitted. "If I hear anything, see anything, or even just think of anything you haven't already thought of, I'll be sure to give you a call."

"Thank you. I appreciate that."

After I clicked off, I continued toward the house. By the time the dogs and I arrived, Mom was up and had coffee made. I still had some time before Trevor would arrive, so I decided to go through the photos I'd taken yesterday and select the best ones to transfer into a file from which I'd choose the photos to be used in the contest. I kissed Mom good morning, poured myself a cup of coffee, and then headed upstairs to the studio I'd set up. I uploaded the photos to my computer and began to sift through them.

There were several totally precious photos of the boy with the puppy before the boy's father had called him to leave. I'd captured an image of two sisters, maybe five and seven, sharing a laugh while they built a snowman. There were a lot of happy families looking for the perfect tree, but none stood out as any better than the others. The photos of people drinking hot cocoa and shopping in the Dooley's Farm gift shop were nice as well, but again not really outstanding.

And then I came across the photo I'd taken of the woman with the dark hair that I'd noticed at the tree farm looking in our direction. She seemed familiar, yet I didn't think I'd never met her. She had dark hair that hung straight from a baseball-style cap. She had sunglasses on, so I couldn't really see what she was looking at, but there was just something about her that gave me the chills. I saved the image to my desktop and moved on to the photos taken at the park. The faces of the children as they watched the mechanical bears, penguins, raccoons, and deer were simply magical. I selected a few of my favorites and transferred them to the folder. I moved on to the photos of couples walking in the park and selected one of an older woman sitting alone feeding the seagulls.

It was then that I noticed a woman standing in the background. She was the same woman I'd seen at Dooley's Farm. Coincidence? Maybe. Both the tree farm and the park were Christmas themed attractions, so if she, like me, had been looking to enjoy everything that Cutter's Cove had to offer during the holidays, I supposed she might have been at both locations I had. I created a new file labeled: Dark-haired Woman. I transferred both the photo I'd taken at Dooley's Farm and the one I'd taken at the park into the file. I tried to tell myself that I was just being extra suspicious after Donovan's call, but as hard as I tried to convince myself that the woman was simply a spectator, I couldn't quite shake the churning that had settled deep in my stomach.

Chapter 6

After Trevor arrived, we set out to conquer the next photos on my list. I had to admit there was a part of my mind that was on the lookout for the woman I'd photographed in two different locations yesterday.

"I would still prefer to capture the ice skating at dusk, so let's start with photos of the snowmen in the park and the sleigh rides being offered in town," I suggested. "I did take snowman photos yesterday, but none of them really spoke to me. I'd like to see if I can find an image that makes a statement."

"A statement about snowmen?"

"A statement about childhood innocence and the magic of Christmas," I corrected.

"Ah. That would be awesome. It might be a good idea to capture photos of families passing by in a sleigh as well as photos of the scenery taken from within a sleigh," Trevor suggested.

"I wouldn't mind a sleigh ride. I guess once we do that, we can grab lunch and then head over to the

Santa House. I still need to take shots of the interior. It's too bad the carnival won't be open until Thursday. I need to turn the collage in by the end of the day on Thursday, so I won't have a lot of time to add photos taken after dark, which I'm sure will be spectacular."

Trevor pulled his truck into the town's public parking lot. The sleigh rides loaded just two blocks down, and the park, where I suspected we could find a good selection of snowmen, was only a block further than that.

"Even with all the photos I have planned, I feel I'm going to need something more," I said.

"Like what?"

"I'm not sure, but I suspect there will be a lot of photos of Santa and snowmen and even tree cutting and sleigh rides. What does Cutter's Cove have that will help it to stand out?"

"The boats in the marina," Trevor suggested. "Many of them have been decked out with colorful lights. We could head over there after dark when everything is lit up."

"I like that idea. In fact, quite a few of these shots will be best if captured after dark. The nativity on the wharf is always a hit, as is the Christmas Pageant, although that isn't until after my deadline. I still feel like something is missing, but let's go ahead and shoot what we can and then see what we have."

Trevor opened my door, and I slid out. We'd left the dogs home with Mom today, so I only had my camera bag and tripod to worry about.

"Should we start with the sleigh ride?" Trevor asked.

"Yes, let's."

Given the fact that it was a weekday, there was no line at the sleigh rides like there had been over the weekend. The man offering the service sold us the deluxe package, which included hot cocoa and a ride through town and the forest. Mac, Trevor, and I had taken a ride together more than a decade ago, which turned out to have been one of the best memories of my life. At least my life to date. Hopefully, I had a lot more living to do.

"This is really nice," I said as I snuggled in next to Trevor. I snapped several photos as we rode through town, but I'd pretty much decided the photos of Main would be best if taken after dark, so I planned to focus most of the sleigh ride photos on the scenery as we meandered through the snow-covered forest.

Trevor laced his fingers through mine once I'd set my camera aside and settled in for the ride. "I can't even begin to tell you how many times I've fantasized about doing exactly this with you over the past decade. After you left, I thought you'd come back right away. When you didn't, I feared I'd never see you again."

"I'm sorry. I don't know why I didn't stay in touch. But I'm here now, and I'm not going anywhere. You and Mac are my best friends. I simply can't imagine a life without you."

Trevor put his arm around my shoulder and pulled me close. I closed my eyes and focused on the warmth of his body, the tiny specs of moisture from the snowflakes on my face, and the gentle motion of the sleigh gliding over the snow. I knew I should be busily snapping photos, but in this moment, life seemed perfect.

When we returned to town, we headed to the park. As there had been the previous day, the park was filled with couples walking hand in hand, children playing, and senior citizens feeding the birds. I paused to take photos of a woman who looked to be in her eighties, having what appeared to be a very serious conversation with a little girl standing in front of the bench she was sitting on. The child, who looked to be three or four, was wearing a bright red coat. It occurred to me that the image portrayed would be spectacular if rendered in black and white, with only the child's red coat to add color.

As I snapped photos, I had to wonder what the pair were chatting about. The conversation seemed friendly, and no one looked scared or upset. Still, based on the intent look in the eyes of both the woman and the girl, it seemed obvious they weren't talking about something causal like Santa or Christmas wishes. Perhaps the woman was related to the girl in some way. Maybe she was telling her a story, or perhaps she was conveying news that was important to both of them.

After a few minutes, the girl leaned forward and whispered something in the woman's ear. The woman hugged her, and then the child walked away. I stopped to see where the child was going. She seemed much too young to be alone. After a moment, she joined a woman with two young children in the playground. I assumed the woman was her mother or maybe her babysitter. I was about to move on when I noticed the same woman with dark hair I'd seen yesterday watching from a distance.

"Do you see that woman with the dark hair standing behind the swings?" I asked Trevor.

He looked where I'd indicated. "Yeah. What about her?"

"I saw her twice yesterday. At least twice. I have a photo of her at the tree farm and another in the park."

"Maybe she's just out enjoying the holiday atmosphere like we are."

"Maybe." Trevor didn't know about the second text, and I didn't plan to tell him. "Let's check out the ice skaters. I'd love to get some shots later in the day, but there might be some pretty wonderful shots to be had now as well."

Chapter 7

By the time the sun set on Cutter's Cove, I had photos of families in sleighs, children building snowmen in the park, couples walking hand in hand, and ice skaters gliding to carols of the season. It had been a fun day, a productive day, a day I was sure I'd remember for a very long time.

"So, what do we have left?" Trevor asked.

"Just the interior of the Santa House, the nativity, the boats in the marina, and the lights in the park and along Main."

"Let's head to the park and the Santa House now. Then we can view the lights on Main and in the marina, take some photos of the nativity, have dinner, and then maybe we can head back to my place. I have a really good bottle of wine just waiting for someone to drink it."

I stood on my tiptoes and kissed Trevor on the cheek. "That sounds perfect. I'd say we could walk, but it is getting cold. There should be parking closer to Santa's Village, so maybe we should just drive to the Santa House."

There was actually a pretty long line by the time we arrived at Santa's Village and the Santa House. Parking wasn't as easy as I thought it would be, but Trevor managed to find a spot. Once we'd parked, we headed toward the crowded building where Santa was holding court. I was actually looking forward to the shifts in the Santa House Trevor and I had signed up for later in the week.

"There isn't a lot of room in here," Trevor said. "Maybe I should stand off to the side while you get the shots you need."

"I think we have a problem," I said.

"Oh. And what is that?"

"A woman is standing behind Santa."

Trevor looked in the direction I indicated. "I don't see anyone behind Santa."

"That's because the woman I'm looking at is a ghost."

"Holly?" he asked.

I nodded. "Go outside and call Woody. Tell him what's going on. It's too crowded in here to talk to the woman. We need to clear the place out or figure out a way to get her to move to a more secluded location."

"I'll call Woody while you try to make contact. Maybe she can move to another location. If not, then we'll look at clearing the building. If nothing else, I can pull the fire alarm."

I nodded and headed toward the front of the room. The line to see Santa was long, and I was willing to bet that there were children who'd been waiting for hours. I really hoped we didn't need to clear everyone out before they got the chance to share their holiday wishes. Holly was standing behind Santa, looking toward the crowd that had come to see him. I made my way around to the back of the Santa chair, so I was standing next to her. I turned to face the wall and not the crowd and took out my phone. I'd decided that I was going to pretend to be on my phone while I tried to make contact with Holly. People were probably going to think I was rude for chatting on my phone with my back to the room, but at least they wouldn't think I was crazy for talking to myself.

"Holly," I said in a voice barely louder than a whisper.

"You can see me?"

"I can."

"Thank goodness. I have been trying to find someone who can see me for the longest time." Her look of relief quickly turned to concern. "Why can you see me?"

"I can see ghosts."

She looked down at her hands. "And I'm a ghost?"

I nodded. "I'm afraid so. It's going to be hard to talk in here. Can you leave?"

"No. I tried to leave several times, but every time I try to walk out the door, I end up back here in this exact same spot."

"Okay. I am going to try to get ahold of someone who can help you. Stay right here, and I'll be back." I pushed my way back through the crowd and headed toward the door. Once outside, I found Trevor. He shared that Woody was on his way, and I shared my intent to try to find Alyson one more time. I found a quiet place away from the line, closed my eyes, and focused.

"Alyson. Can you hear me? I need your help. We have a ghost that needs our help."

I was afraid she wouldn't appear, so I felt a huge amount of relief when she did.

"Did you call for me?" she asked.

"I've been calling for you since yesterday. Haven't you heard?"

She paused as if thinking over my question. "No, I guess not. Do you need something?"

"We have a ghost to help. Her name is Holly, and she's inside the Santa House."

"I take it she's a new ghost?"

"I found her body yesterday, and I suspect she died in the overnight hours of the previous night. She knows she's a ghost. I told her as much. She can't leave the Santa House, and there are a ton of people inside. I need to know if she knows what happened to her."

"What did happen to her?" Alyson asked.

"We're still waiting for the official cause of death, but it looks like she may have overdosed. There are a lot of variables at play here, and I really need to talk to her to see if she knows what happened. If you talk to her, I can stand there quietly and listen to her replies. No one will think anything about it as long as it doesn't look like I'm talking to myself."

"Okay. You want me to ask her if she remembers what happened. Anything else?"

"Find out if she remembers who she was with. She was at a bar before she died, but we don't know where she went or who she might have been with after she left the bar. And I have no idea how she ended up in the Santa House. Also, ask her if she's ready to move on. I suppose we should make sure she does that before she gets stuck here."

"Okay. I'm on it."

Alyson disappeared, and I headed back inside. Trevor was waiting outside for Woody. I hoped that by the time he arrived, we'd have some answers.

"Holly, I'm Alyson," she introduced herself as I stood nearby.

"You look just like the other one, but you're a ghost. Are you twins?"

"No, not twins, and I'm not a ghost exactly," Alyson replied. "It's a long story. Listen, Amanda wants me to ask you if you remember what happened to you."

She paused but didn't answer right away. Eventually, she spoke. "I don't know. It's all a little fuzzy."

"What do you remember?"

She narrowed her gaze. "I was working here at the Santa House with Owen. I remember I had a date with a real estate agent I met a few weeks ago. I wanted to buy a house, and he was going to help me, so we were going to meet to talk about it. Owen noticed I had heels on, so he offered to drop me off at the bar on his way home."

"Okay, so walk me through what happened after you arrived at the bar," Alyson said.

"Chris was already there. He ordered me a drink, and we chatted. I guess we must have been on our second drink when Chris got a call about some sort of problem at one of his listings. He said he had to leave and asked me if I needed a ride home. I told him that I was going to stay for a while and would just call a friend."

"And then?" Alyson asked.

"And then I went to the ladies' room. When I came back, the bartender had made me another drink, so I sat there and chatted with him for a while."

"Do you know the bartender?" Alyson asked.

"As well as anyone can know a bartender. I know his name is Dave, and he's worked at the bar for a long time. The bar is close to where I live and work, so I stop by and have a drink sometimes, and we chat."

"Do you remember what you chatted about on the night you died?"

She slowly shook her head. "I don't remember. It's all sort of blurry."

"One of the cocktail waitresses who works at The Rusty Nail said that she ran into you in the ladies' room, and you told her you didn't feel well. Do you remember that?"

"No. I don't remember talking to anyone in the ladies' room, but I do remember feeling strange at some point. I remember wanting to leave. I'm not sure what happened after that."

I nodded to Alyson. She seemed to understand and nodded back.

"We're going to go outside for a few minutes. We need to discuss some things," Alyson said. "But we'll be back, and after we ask a few more questions, I'll help you move on."

"You can do that?"

Alyson nodded. "I think I can. Wait right here."

With that, I headed toward the door once again. When I exited the building, I saw Trevor chatting with Woody. I walked to where they were standing and filled them in.

"I'm hoping that with some prompting, Holly will remember what happened," I added. "Alyson can talk to her without being overheard, so maybe we just need to come up with the right questions to stimulate her memory."

We chatted about what questions Alyson should ask, and then she and I headed back inside. Holly was still standing in the same spot I'd found her when we first arrived.

"You came back," she said.

"I said we would," Alyson replied. "We have a few more questions."

"Okay. I'll tell you what I can."

"At some point on the night you died, you came into contact with some pretty powerful drugs. Had you taken drugs in the past?" Alyson asked.

"No. Never. I like to go out and have a few drinks, but I don't do drugs. I swear."

"We think you might have been drugged while you were in the bar. That's probably why you started to feel strange. Do you have any idea who might have put drugs in your drink?" Alyson asked.

Holly slowly shook her head back and forth. "I'm not sure. I can't really remember."

"If you wanted to leave and needed a ride, who would you have called?"

"One of my roommates."

"You live with four men?"

She nodded.

"Are you close? Have you known them long?" Alyson asked.

"No. I met them shortly before moving in with them. I was in an auto accident a while back and lost my job. I had no money and nowhere to live, but I met this guy in a bar. We got to talking, and he told me he had an extra room in the house where he lived and offered to let me stay with him and his roommates."

"And you became friends."

"We did. All four of my roommates are really nice, and I am happy for the roof over my head, but they are total slobs. I was recently given an advance on a potential settlement from a lawsuit I'm involved in and decided to use it to buy a small house, which is how I met Chris."

"Potential settlement?" I asked, even though I knew it was best to remain quiet.

"The lawsuit from the auto accident I was in has turned into this whole big thing. I told my attorney that I just wanted him to settle since I needed cash to pay my bills, but he kept insisting that we needed to hold out for the big payday. When I threatened to find another attorney who could get me cash now, rather than later, he gave me an advance. It's only a small portion of what he insists we can expect to receive, but it was enough to pay my overdue bills and find a place to live, so I accepted. I have a new job now, which helps with the day to day expenses."

Alyson looked at me after Holly stopped talking. I nodded. "Since you are trapped here in the Santa House, it seems to indicate that you died here. Do you remember coming here?"

She looked around. "I'm not sure. I need to think about it. I do volunteer here a lot, so I have the door code. It's warm and safe, so I suppose that if I needed somewhere to hang out for a while, I might have come here. But if I did come here, I don't remember what happened."

"You had on high heels when we found your body. You couldn't have walked here. Could you have called someone for a ride?" I whispered, hoping that no one would notice that I was talking to no one.

She paused and then answered. "I remember being in the bar. I remember having a drink and talking to Dave, and then the next thing I remember is waking up here in the Santa House. I don't know how I got here, but I do remember that when I woke up, no one was here. After a while, people started showing up. That was when I tried to speak to them, but no one could hear me. No one other than you and Alyson." A look of panic crossed her face. "It's important that I remember what happened to me. Right? That's why you're here talking to me. No one knows what happened, and you are hoping I do. But I don't. I want to help, but everything is such a blur."

"Okay, just relax," Alyson said. "Just let the memories come to you. Don't try to force them, and don't try to make sense out of what you remember. Just let them come."

"Okay." She closed her eyes.

Alyson continued. "You remember waking up in the Santa House. Now, try to remember how you got here. You didn't have a car, so you must have gotten a ride. Try to picture yourself in the car. Try to focus on who you're with."

"I don't remember a car, but I do remember feeling sick. I was going to call a friend, but then I decided to call Uber," she frowned, "but I didn't."

"Do you remember why you didn't?"

She hesitated. “I didn’t have my phone. I remember wanting to call for a car, but I didn’t have my phone.” Her eyes flew open. “I’d left it here. I remembered that Owen had needed to make a call and his phone was dead, so I let him use mine. I must have forgotten to get it back.”

“So, what did you do after you realized that you didn’t have your phone?” Alyson asked.

“I asked Dave if I could use the phone at the bar.”

“Dave is the bartender.” Alyson verified.

“Yes. I told him what happened and asked to use the phone. He said I could, but then Rowen said he was heading out and offered to bring me back here to get my phone.”

“And who is Rowen?”

“He owns the bar.”

“And did he drop you here, or did he take you somewhere else?” Alyson asked.

She took a moment to consider her answer. “He must have dropped me here. I don’t remember him dropping me here, but I also don’t remember going anywhere else.” She paused. “I remember him offering to bring me here, and then I remember waking up, but nothing in between.”

“And where were you when you woke up?” Alyson asked. “Where exactly?”

“I was sitting in the Santa chair,” she said. “I remember waking up and feeling dizzy. More than dizzy. I felt like the ceiling was falling, and the room was closing in on me. I remember that I was terrified, and I felt like I needed to find a way to prop up the building before it collapsed on me. Things were moving and spinning, and I was pretty sure I was going to be sick, but then I heard voices coming from the other side of the door. I remember holding my breath as someone tried to open the door."

"Did whoever you heard have a key?"

"There's a keypad that must be accessed to get in. I remember that the person trying to open the door was having a hard time and had to try several times before the door opened. I remember being scared, so I ran and hid in the dressing room."

"Do you remember anything else?" Alyson asked.

"I remember crouching on the floor in the dressing room. I remember listening as someone walked around outside the door to the small room. I don't remember anything after that until the lady who cleans came in. I tried to talk to her, but she acted like I wasn't even here. I thought that was odd but wasn't completely freaked out until I realized no one could see or hear me. Not until Amanda came in, that is."

"Do you remember seeing your body at any point after you left it?" Alyson asked.

"No. I don't remember seeing my body, and I don't remember what happened after I went into the dressing room to hide." She looked at Alyson. "You said you could help me move on."

She nodded. "If you are ready, I can take you part of the way."

Holly looked at me. "This is really freaking me out, and there really isn't a reason for me to stay. I would like to know what happened to me, but it sounds like it isn't going to be an easy thing to figure out, and I really just want to forget about the whole thing."

Amanda placed a hand on her arm. "It is true that it may take a while to track down any clues that exist. And I agree that you should go if you are ready."

She looked at Alyson. “I am ready.” She turned and looked at me. “I hope you find your answers.”

Alyson took her hand, and they disappeared. I wasn’t sure when Alyson might appear again. Sometimes these things took a lot of time, while other times, she returned fairly quickly. I felt bad that we hadn’t been able to give Holly her answers, but she appeared to be ready to move on, and there really was no reason to keep her from finding the peace she seemed to be seeking.

Chapter 8

Woody decided to close the Santa House and call in the crime scene unit. Now that we strongly suspected that Holly had died within the walls of the building, Woody felt it was important to go through the place with a fine-tooth comb, even though any evidence that may have existed was most likely compromised by this point. The parents and children who'd waited in line but hadn't gotten to see Santa weren't happy, but Woody did what he needed to do anyway.

Trevor and I headed into town to have dinner and take the photos of the lights we'd come to take. It was difficult to transition from chatting with a ghost who'd recently been murdered to enjoying the Christmas festivities Cutter's Cove had to offer, but once we'd been walking around looking at window displays for a while, we both started to relax.

"There's a line out the door at the toy store," I said as we walked along the sidewalk that was lined on one side by festively decorated windows, and by trees decorated with white twinkle lights on the other side.

"Christmas is just around the corner. Have you finished your shopping?"

"I did most of it online this year," I answered. "I do enjoy the hustle and bustle associated with hitting the stores to look for the perfect gift, but this year things seemed busy. First, we had the cruise, and then there was the shooting of the social worker to help with. It's nice to walk around and look at the lights and the stores without the added pressure of needing to find gifts. How about you? Have you finished your shopping?" I asked Trevor.

"I'm actually making some of my gifts this year. Those I had to mail have already been sent off except the one for my father."

I leaned my head on his shoulder. "That's right. You told me that you were making a desk for Mac. How is that going?"

"It turned out really well. I just have one final coat of clear lacquer to add, and it will be done. I think she's really going to like it. I had to call Ty and ask him about the electrical panel. I wanted Mac to have all the plugs and ports she would need. He was actually very helpful. I'm glad Mac decided to take a chance and go out with the guy. He seems like a good fit for our little group."

"I agree. Ty is great." I pulled Trevor into a candy store. "I'm going to buy my mom some divinity. Our cook used to make it every year, and I know Mom really looked forward to it."

"Does this cook still work for your mom?"

"No. She passed away a few years ago. My mom has a meal service now. She goes out to eat a lot, and didn't feel that she really needed a full-time staff person once Cookie passed."

"Your cook's name was Cookie?"

"Nickname. Her actual name was Ursula."

Trevor pulled out his wallet and paid for the candy. It was a nice gesture, but I felt like I needed to figure out a way so he wouldn't pay for everything. I had old family money to draw on, which wasn't likely to run out in my lifetime, while he had to work for every penny he had.

"I need to stop by the clock shop as long as we're here," Trevor said after he handed me the bag of candy he'd just paid for.

"Are you buying a clock?"

"Actually, I'm having a watch repaired. It was my grandfather's. My father always admired it, but it has been broken since before Grandpa died, so I asked my mom to send it to me. I've had it completely restored and plan to send it to him for Christmas."

"Aw. That is a sweet and thoughtful gift. I'm sure he'll love it."

"I hope so. He's a hard man to buy for."

"There's a jewelry store next to the clock shop. I saw a pair of earrings in there a few days ago that I might buy for my mom."

Shopping with Trevor was really special. Walking hand in hand while we looked at the displays, purchasing odds and ends, and talking about Christmas dreams past and present was wonderful. As there had been all week, tiny flakes of snow were in the air. I knew the flurries wouldn't amount to much in terms of additional snow depth, but it certainly added a festive element to the evening.

Once I'd captured all the photos I wanted to take of the lights downtown, we headed toward the wharf. I wanted to photograph the nativity and the boats in the marina that many of the owners had lit up for the season, and then we planned to go to dinner at the restaurant at the end of the wooden structure. I was just finishing up with the last of the photos when we ran into Caleb Wellington and Chelsea Green. Trevor and I had gone to high school with Caleb and Chelsea, and while Chelsea hadn't been one of my favorite people back then, she'd grown into a woman I liked and admired.

"Isn't the marina spectacular?" Chelsea asked, hugging Caleb's arm.

"It really is breathtaking. Will they do the Christmas Eve boat parade this year?" I wondered.

"If the weather cooperates," Chelsea answered. "So, I heard about Holly," she jumped right in, the way she was prone to do. "I'm sorry to hear about her death, but it sounds like there are a whole lot of people who are happy that she's no longer causing trouble for the town council."

"Town council?" This is the first I'd heard about Holly having a conflict with the town council.

"Holly was injured in a hit and run last winter. She recovered and looked fine, but she almost died and was in the hospital for over a month."

"I heard that she'd been in an accident and was involved in a lawsuit, but what does that have to do with the town council?"

Chelsea nodded. "The intersection where she was struck has a blind corner, and I will admit it has seen more than its share of accidents in spite of the yield signs warning motorists to slow down and proceed carefully. Anyway, one of the residents who lives in the neighborhood has been campaigning for years to have the intersection monitored with a traffic light. This particular resident has been insisting that it was only a matter of time until a serious accident occurred and that it was the town's duty to take precautions."

"It does sound like the corner should have a light," I said.

"I don't disagree, but the residents who live closest to where the light would be installed don't want a light, claiming that a traffic light would shine in their windows and lower their property value. After Holly's accident, one of those personal injury attorneys from Portland contacted Holly and convinced her to sue the town for a whole lot of money."

"Okay, that sounds bad, but not bad enough to kill someone over," I said.

"There's more," Chelsea said. "In addition to suing the town, the attorney who'd contacted Holly decided to sue each and every council member personally since the issue relating to the intersection had been brought up on numerous occasions, but no action had ever been taken. He claims that the council members were negligent, and therefore personally liable."

"Don't council members have insurance for this sort of thing?" I asked.

"They do, but this attorney is going for the jugular. If he can prove negligence, and he gets what he is asking for, insurance won't cover it."

"So, with Holly dead, will the lawsuit go away?" Trevor asked.

"I'm not sure," Chelsea answered. "I know that the attorney trying the case was relying heavily on the jury feeling sympathy for Holly to get the settlement he's looking for. To be honest, I've felt from the beginning that he was using her for a big payday and never really cared about her. I know the town tried offering Holly a settlement that would take care of her medical costs plus a reasonable amount for pain and suffering, and according to several people I've spoken to, Holly was happy with the offer and planned to accept it, but the attorney talked her into going for a big payday."

I narrowed my gaze. "You aren't saying that one of the council members being sued is responsible for her death?"

"What?" Chelsea looked genuinely shocked. "No. Of course, I am not saying that. All I'm saying is that the council must be relieved her testimony is no longer a threat."

Chapter 9

After we'd chatted with Chelsea the previous evening, I called Woody and gave him a heads up about the lawsuit. He, of course, already knew about the case, which had been kept fairly quiet to this point, but like Chelsea, he didn't consider any of the town council members to be suspects in her death. While I didn't want to think that anyone on the town council would kill a young woman over a lawsuit, I couldn't quite get the idea out of my mind that the litigation might still be at the root of whatever was going on.

Trevor and I had enjoyed a nice dinner, but instead of talk of romance or even the Christmas holiday, most of the discussion had revolved around Holly's death and the possible suspects that came to mind. We'd gone through and talked about each of the town council members separately. I'd been gone for a decade and only knew two of the seven. Trevor was familiar with all the men and women on the council and told me what he could about each of them. It seemed that those who ended up on the town council were individuals of wealth. I supposed I could understand the need to protect that wealth from an overzealous attorney, but to resort to murder? I certainly hoped that wasn't what had occurred.

Mac had texted and let me know that she planned to stay in Portland for a few extra days, but would be home by mid-week. Even as I read the text, I knew that it was only a matter of time before she moved out of Cutter's Cove and in with Ty full-time. I didn't really blame her. Ty was a great guy, and there didn't seem to be any reason for them not to continue to move their relationship forward. When I'd spoken to her about it, she'd assured me that she had no plans to move in with Ty anytime soon, but in my opinion, actions spoke louder than words.

After I'd returned from walking the dogs, I decided to work on sorting the photos I'd taken yesterday. I had some with depth and feeling that I knew would work well, but I still felt like I was lacking that special something to tie them all together. When I got to the one I'd taken of the woman with dark hair, I added it to the folder with the other two photos. I wasn't sure why I was so bothered by this woman showing up at three of the locations I had. She wasn't doing anything suspicious in any of the photos, and there were a lot of people mingling around. It was probably just a coincidence that I happened to be snapping photos when she seemed to be looking in my direction.

I wondered if I should call Donovan. Of course, even if I did, what would I say? There seems to be a woman showing up at the same Christmas attractions

I'd decided to photograph. Even he would probably think I'd grown paranoid. To this point, the woman hadn't actually done anything, so after a bit of introspection, I decided to wait and do nothing for the time being.

Trevor planned to work a full day at Pirates Pizza today, so I was on my own. He had a manager that ran things when he wasn't there, as well as a handful of employees, so he did have some flexibility, but since he was open from eleven to nine, Tuesday through Saturday, he had to cover the front at least part of the time. During the summer, he worked a lot of hours, but during the winters, he tended to cover the lunch crowd, and then he would work on advertising, bookkeeping, food orders, and other administrative duties while his manager ran the front from two to nine. The manager would then close and get things ready for Trevor to open the next day. There were exceptions such as last Saturday when Trevor worked the full day to allow his manager a long weekend off.

I went through the photos we'd taken and began working on the arrangement process. I wasn't unhappy with the shots I'd taken the past couple of days, but I really felt that the collage I had so far was just okay. If I was going to have a shot at winning the contest, I needed better than okay. I had to find that one photo, theme, or hook that would turn okay into exceptional.

The photo of the girl with the red jacket talking to the old woman was my favorite. I experimented with different gray tones until I found just the right contrast. I also had the images of the boy with the red jacket playing with the puppy, who was still with me.

Perhaps I'd try using a gray tone on those as well, leaving only the red jacket for contrast. In fact, I decided I'd try doing the entire collage using a gray tone with a splash of red to really set it off.

One of the sailboats in the marina had red and white lights strung along the mast and around the windows of the cabin. I found a snowman with a red scarf, a young boy with a red sled and red hat and gloves, and a couple walking hand in hand with matching red sweaters. The penguins in Santa's Village had red scarves around their necks, as did the polar bears. I went through my photos one more time looking for images that may not have stood out the first time around, but given my current theme might work even better than some I had selected. I'd just come across a wonderful image of a dog running through the park with a red knit scarf in his mouth when my phone rang. It was Woody.

"Hey, what's up?" I answered.

"When you spoke to Holly, did she mention anything about a payment she received from her attorney?" he asked.

"She did. She said that she wanted to settle with the town so she could pay her bills and get back on her feet, but the attorney was adamant that they hold out for the big payday. She said that her attorney arranged for her to have an advance on her anticipated settlement to help her get by in the meantime. Why do you ask?"

"I'm looking into Holly's financial records, and I noticed a large deposit into her account. I guess that must be the deposit from the attorney."

"Did you find anything else?"

"I spoke to Dave, the bartender, and Rowen, the owner of The Rusty Nail. Both admit to speaking to Holly on the night she died, but neither claim to know how she might have ended up with drugs in her system or where she went after she left the bar."

"Holly said that the bar owner gave her a ride."

"I remembered you said that, so I asked him about it. I told him that a spectator had seen him giving Holly a ride, but he denied it. He said the spectator must have seen someone else. I couldn't very well tell him that it was Holly who gave me that piece of information, so I can't prove anything at this point, but I will say that Rowen Morton is my prime suspect. Not only did he have access to her drink, but he is part of the lawsuit Holly was involved in, so he had a motive as well.

"How was he part of the lawsuit?"

"Rowen Morton was on the town council."

"Trevor and I discussed the town council members and I don't remember his mentioning anyone by that name."

"That's probably because Morton is no longer on the town council. He resigned after the lawsuit was filed and was replaced by Francine Rutgers. But he was on the council when the suit was filed and is still listed as a defendant."

Ah, the plot thickens. "If the bar owner is part of the lawsuit it does sound like he makes a good suspect. It appears he had both motive and opportunity. Still, something about the whole thing feels off to me. Holly said she heard voices coming from the other side of the door that scared her, and when someone tried to open the door, it caused her to run and hide. She said that before the door was opened, she had been passed out in the Santa chair. That indicates to me she was already safely deposited in the Santa House before the people she ran and hid from entered. If this is true, even if the bar owner did give her a ride, it sounds as if she was still alive after he dropped her off."

"That's true. I wonder why he would lie about giving her a ride if he didn't kill her."

"That part really doesn't make sense unless he just wants to distance himself from the whole thing. He must know that he is going to be a suspect. Holly had been in his bar before her death, and she had been involved in a lawsuit that stood to cost him a whole lot of money. Maybe he was afraid to admit that he was most likely the last person to see her alive."

"He wasn't the last person unless he's the one who broke in after Holly was already in the Santa House. We really need to figure out who Holly heard that night."

"Based on what Holly said, it sounds as if one of the people who broke in had the code to the door of the Santa House," I pointed out. "Holly said it took the person trying to open the door a few tries, but that they did get in using the keypad."

I could hear Woody breathing over the phone line. He wasn't speaking, so I assumed he was considering the situation.

"Okay," he eventually said. "It sounds like we need to get a list of the people who have the code."

"Trevor and I are volunteering at the Santa House this weekend. I asked about access and was told that the code is reset several times a week to try to keep the building secure. The event coordinator is supposed to text me the code on Saturday morning. If the code is reset every few days, the number of people with a particular code that will open the door will be limited. Of course, there is no guarantee that someone who was given the code didn't pass it along to someone who wasn't authorized to have it, but a list would be a good place to start."

"I'll call the coordinator and get one."

Woody and I spoke for a few more minutes, and then I hung up. I really wanted to decide on a theme for my collage by the end of the day. The red with the gray tone was striking, but I just wasn't sure. My mom was an artist, so I decided to get her opinion.

"The gray tone with the red elements really does pop, but it doesn't necessarily give me the feeling of warmth I associate with a small-town Christmas," she said after I'd shown her a sample of what I was thinking.

"Yeah," I sighed. "I agree. I saw the photo of the young girl talking to the old woman and the image really resonated with me. I loved the pop of red once I manipulated the colors a bit, but a whole collage done in the same theme doesn't really convey the feeling I'm after."

"Why did you like that photo in the first place?" Mom asked.

I looked at it carefully. "I guess it was the expression on both the young girl and the old woman's faces. They look so serious, yet you can sense affection as well. Something about their interaction really pulled me in. I have a lot of fun photos of boats with Christmas lights and lopsided snowmen that make me think of Christmas, but the image of the young girl with the old woman in the park causes me to linger. It makes me want to know more about what was being said and what sort of relationship the two might share."

"So, maybe that's your theme. The Faces of Christmas. Let the people you capture tell the story of why Christmas in Cutter's Cove is so special."

I paused to think about this for a moment. "I really like that idea. The photo of the boy with the puppy works as well." I pointed to the photo. "Look at that face. He is totally into the moment. In spite of the fact that he was trying to get his sled up the hill and it kept sliding back down each time the puppy jumped on him, you just know he wouldn't have wanted it any other way." I stood up and hugged my mom. "Thanks for the feedback. I'm going to go up and look through the photos again. I'm going to eliminate the images that don't have people in them and try to focus on the emotion of the season as seen on the faces of those we come in contact with at this time of the year."

Mom got up and refilled her coffee. "I'm helping out with the candy making for the town fundraiser. In fact, I'm not even sure if I'll be back for dinner. I'll text you and let you know."

"Okay. Have fun."

I spent the next few hours going through the photos I'd taken once again. I tried to find those images that best represented my new theme. I did like the new direction the collage was taking, but I knew I was still missing a few key photos that I felt I needed to round things out. I decided to grab my camera and head into town. It was a weekday, so there wouldn't be as many people out and about, but there would be women at the community center making candy, a crew should be starting to set up the Christmas

Carnival, and the Santa House might be open by now. I supposed I'd just stop by and check.

Since Trevor and I had arranged to meet for a late dinner after he got off work, I made a sandwich to tide me over, took the dogs for a quick run, and then headed into town. I decided to start in the park. There were always people mingling around, and if the Santa House had reopened, I might be able to get some good shots there. When I arrived, I found Woody standing in front of the house, looking at the doorway. The frown on his face indicated to me that his thoughts were troubled.

"Penny for your thoughts?" I asked, walking up beside him.

"I'm just trying to work through the timeline as presented by Holly and narrow down the window for the time of death. It sounds as if she went to the bar right after her shift. I checked, and the Santa House closed at eight that night. I also spoke to one of the cocktail waitresses who works at The Rusty Nail on Friday and Saturday nights, and she confirmed that Holly did meet Chris around eight-thirty and that they sat at the bar. She thought Holly might have left at around ten. I realize that people metabolize drugs differently, but based on what I've learned about the specific drug found in Holly's system, it sounds like it would take around thirty minutes for her to begin to feel its effects. If she was slipped the drug at the bar and began to feel dizzy before she left, I am going to estimate she ingested the drug between nine and nine-thirty. It seems that if the bar owner did give her a ride to the Santa House, and she passed out after she arrived only to be awakened later by the people who entered, he probably isn't the one who killed her. He could have come back, but I'm not sure why he would do that."

"Do you have the official cause of death yet? Is it possible that she died as a result of the drugs in her system, and no one actually killed her?"

"I considered that option, but decided that if she died as the result of an overdose, there would have been no reason for anyone to move the body."

"I suppose that's true. Go on. You were wondering about the timeline."

"I remembered that you told me that Holly shared that she had first attempted to speak to the cleaning lady. It sounds like she was already a ghost at that point since the cleaning lady was unable to see her."

"Yes, that is correct," I confirmed. "She said the cleaning lady came in and she tried to speak to her but was unable to. That was when she began to suspect something was wrong."

"I called and spoke to the woman who is contracted to clean the Santa House. She does a graveyard shift, and she told me she arrived at the Santa House around midnight."

"So, the timeline between when Holly left the bar and when she realized she was dead was only about two hours. And if the cleaning lady didn't find the body, the person who moved it must have already done so."

"It sounds like the timeline is pretty tight. Did you get a list of everyone who would have had a door code on the day Holly died?"

"I did."

He handed it to me. There were only eleven people on the list.

"The code changed on Friday morning and was due to change again on Monday, so the only people who were given the new code were the support personnel for the weekend, the event organizers, and the Santas and elves volunteering Friday through Sunday," Woody explained. "There were two crews per day, although Holly and Owen had shifts two of the three days, and Steve Henderson and Claudia Brown had shifts all three days, so there were only three different teams in all. That's six people. The other five people listed are the event coordinator, the Santa House supervisor, the girl taking the photos, the woman working the counter in the Santa house, and the cleaning lady."

"Have you spoken to these people?"

"All but two. Claudia Brown did a late morning and early afternoon shift with Steve Henderson on Friday. She said that Holly and Owen showed up right on time to take over for her and Steve. After she left the Santa house, she picked her kids up from school, and then they all went to the mall in Portland to start their Christmas shopping. They didn't get home until after eleven, at which time she put her kids to bed and then went to bed herself."

Woody took a breath and then continued. "The cleaning lady confirmed that she arrived at the Santa House around midnight and was done cleaning by one. She worked until five a.m., slept until noon, and then went to her part-time job at the laundromat. After she got off work at the laundromat, she began her graveyard shift cleaning businesses in the area. She doesn't have an alibi for the time Holly died since she was cleaning the Santa House, and no one was around, but in a way, Holly provided an alibi, so

I don't suspect her. The third Santa and elf team, Monica Right and Evan Smith, didn't work on Friday. I did ask both for alibis for Friday between ten p.m. and midnight. Monica told me she was home with her family, while Evan told me he played poker with his Friday night group. I have since confirmed this."

"So, that leaves Owen and Steve," I said. "Along with the event coordinator, the woman who took the photos, the woman who worked the counter, and the Santa House supervisor."

"The same women took photos and worked the counter the entire weekend. Both have alibis for the evening Holly died and I have no reason to suspect either. I haven't managed to track down either Steve or Owen, but I left messages for both of them. The event coordinator is a woman named Pamela Cobalter. She said she was at home fast asleep during the window when Holly died. I really have no reason to suspect her."

"And the Santa House supervisor?" I asked.

"A woman named Jessica Valdez." Woody paused before he continued. "I'm not sure about her. She didn't have an alibi other than being home alone, and I got a strange vibe when I spoke to her. I felt like she was lying about something, but I just wasn't sure if she was lying about her role in Holly's death or if she was lying about something else. I did some checking, and she's had some unusual activity in her personal finances. She seems to have been suffering financially, and there was evidence that she was so far behind on her mortgage that she was in danger of losing her home, and then seemingly out of nowhere, regular deposits began to show up in her bank account beginning about the time the Santa House opened for the season."

"Do you think those deposits are related to what happened to Holly?"

"I don't know. I asked her about them, and she told me that she had taken on a second job to try to make ends meet. I asked for contact information for her employer, and she told me she was being paid under the table and had promised not to tell anyone about the arrangement."

"Seems like a suspiciously convenient reason for not giving you that information," I pointed out.

"I agree. I'm going to continue to poke around. If I feel like I have a good enough reason to subpoena the information, I will. It also occurred to me that the second job might just be a cover for embezzlement. Ms. Valdez handles all the administrative functions for the Santa House, including the bookkeeping."

"I suppose that makes sense as well. Do you think that Holly realized what Jessica was doing and called her on it, so Jessica killed her to keep her secret?"

"That explanation makes sense too. There is something else that I'm toying with, but really don't have much of a foothold on at this point."

"And what is that?" I asked.

"When I was here Saturday after you found Holly's body, I noticed that there were boxes and boxes of snow globes in the storage room. When I came back the following day for a second look, the snow globes were gone. I asked Ms. Valdez about it, and she told me the globes were defective, and she sent them back. I didn't think a lot about it at the time, but after I noticed the deposits to Ms. Valdez's bank account, I began to wonder if the missing snow globes were a clue."

"Do you think she is stealing stuff?"

"The thought occurred to me, but I don't think she is necessarily stealing snow globes. I think she might be the middleman in the smuggling of precious gems."

My brow narrowed. "Okay, you'll need to walk me through that."

"The globes were real fancy inside. I noticed that a lot of gemstones were used as ornaments on the trees, and diamonds were sparkling in the snow. Of course, it is likely the stones are simply colored glass, but given the deposits to Ms. Valdez's account and the fact that there were dozens of boxes of snow globes one day and they were gone the next, I have to wonder if there might be something more going on."

"Did you ask her for an invoice?" I wondered.

"I did. She has an invoice for three dozen cases of snow globes from a company called Baylor Enterprises, and a matching invoice for the return of three dozen cases of snow globes. It appears that the snow globes were shipped from Baylor Enterprises' warehouse in China, but they were returned to their warehouse in Seattle."

"So, the snow globes might be a way to smuggle precious gems into the country."

"Maybe. I don't have any proof at this point, but it is a theory, and it might explain the deposits to Ms. Valdez's bank account."

"So, maybe Holly figured out what was going on, and Valdez killed her."

Woody shrugged. "I don't know. It is a theory, but it's not the only theory. If Valdez is the killer, that could explain the voices. She would have had the code, and perhaps she and a helper or even her buyer were either picking up or dropping off shipments of whatever she was laundering at the time."

"So, do you think she's done this before?" I asked.

"I think she may have done this before if that's even what she's doing. I found that in addition to the snow globes, she purchased four cases of Santa figurines from Baylor Enterprises. The timing of that fits better with the timeline relating to Holly's death."

"Did she claim to have returned them as well?"

"No. She said they weren't as cute as expected, so she sold them for cost to a curio shop in Seattle. She had an invoice that makes it appear that is what occurred, but…"

"But it does sound like there are a lot of cash neutral transactions going on. Do you have a plan to prove this one way or another?"

"Not really. If Valdez is acting as the middleman for illegal property, I doubt that she'll continue to run the items through the store in the Santa House now that she knows I'm snooping around. I made a call to a guy I know who works for Interpol. I figure that if merchandise is being moved from one country to another by illegal means, he might want to know about it. If Valdez killed Holly to cover up her side business, I will prove that, but it isn't really my job to get wrapped up in illegal trade."

"Yeah. I get that. So, it sounds like your suspect list in terms of Holly's murder is Rowen Morton since Holly was suing him and Jessica Valdez if you're correct and she's running illegal goods through the Santa House and Holly found out about it."

"At this point, that's about it. I still need to track down Owen and Steve, which I think I'll go and do now."

Chapter 10

While Woody was busy tracking down suspects, I decided to try to get some additional photos for my project. I headed over to the ice rink where carols were blaring, and happy skaters slid gracefully, or not, around the rink. The laughter and smiles were plentiful, so I suspected that I'd end up with some keepers from all the shots I'd taken. I was swaying to the music and considering the idea of heading home for my own skates when I noticed the same dark-haired woman I'd been noticing the past few days sitting on a bench on the far side of the rink watching the skaters as I was. She wasn't doing anything suspicious, so I had no reason to find her presence suspicious, but there was just something about her that I found unsettling.

I snapped another photo of her. My fourth. Perhaps I was the stalker in this situation.

On a whim, I attached the photo I'd taken to a text and sent it to Donovan. I casually mentioned that I kept running into the woman and was beginning to think I was being followed. I shared that she looked familiar and asked if he recognized her. He said he didn't, but he was glad I'd texted since he needed to talk to me. He asked if I was free to talk, and when I said I was, he called me.

"Do you have more news?" I asked.

"I received another text an hour ago on the phone that belongs to you. The text is a photo of you. Nothing else. Just the photo. The background is blurry and nondescript, but I hoped you would be able to tell me when and where it was taken."

"Yeah. I might be able to do that. I'll put you on speaker. Text it to me, and I'll take a look."

He did as I asked. I heard a ding and popped over to my texting app. "Oh, my," I said in a shaky tone of voice.

"What is it?" Donovan asked.

"The photo was taken yesterday. I'm standing in front of one of the seasonal buildings down by the wharf. Trevor and I went to dinner there last night. I'm alone, so this must have been shot when he went inside to check on our table."

I stopped talking and expected Donovan to reply, but my explanation about the photo was met with silence.

"Donovan? Did I lose you?"

"No. I'm here. The text was sent to the phone registered to you from the same burner number the threating texts have been sent from. The fact that this person took this photo yesterday means that he or she knows you're in Oregon and not New York, and it means that he or she is there in Oregon with you."

"Do you think I am in danger?"

"I think you might be. Maybe you should go home and stay there until I can get this sorted out."

"No. If this person wanted me dead, I'd already be dead. I'll keep my eyes open, but I am not going to run and hide. If you get any new information, call me. In the meantime, can we leave Mom out of this? You know how she worries."

"I think she has the right to know what's going on."

"Maybe, but I'd rather wait and talk to her when I have something tangible to share."

"Okay, I won't say anything for now. I'm going to follow up on some things, and I'll call you later in the day."

After I hung up with Donovan, I headed toward Pirates Pizza. I had a lot of thoughts running through my mind, and I felt like I needed to talk things through with someone who already knew what was going on. Trevor was working in the kitchen today, so I pulled up a stool and chatted while he made pizzas.

"Woody is following up with everyone who had access to the code that opened the door to the Santa House," I informed him. "There weren't a lot of people with the code, but it did sound like the person who accessed the Santa House had the code, so it makes sense it was one of the people on the list. He has a suspicion relating to the Santa House supervisor, a woman named Jessica Valdez." I then shared the information Woody had provided me about the deposits into her account and the strange inventory.

"Wow. It sounds like Woody might really have stumbled onto something," Trevor said.

"I agree, although if she killed Holly, I don't know how the drugging fits into the whole thing."

"Maybe it doesn't," Trevor spread sauce on the dough he'd just shaped into a round. "We still don't know for certain that the person who drugged her is the one who killed her."

"It would be too absurd if there were two different people involved." I paused to think through the scenario. "Still, unless we have the timing wrong, the timeline does seem to suggest that."

Trevor pulled a bowl with dough out of the refrigerator and began making rounds. "It sounds like she began feeling funny while she was still at the bar, indicating that she was most likely drugged at the bar. We have intel that suggests that the bar owner gave her a ride to the Santa House, although he is not admitting that. Still, if he did give her a ride, why not just kill her then? It makes no sense that he would drop her off and leave and then come back later and kill her."

"That's true."

"And for the rest to have happened, for Holly to have fallen asleep and then been awoken by someone trying to get in, she would have had to have been left there. If she did hear the voices and hide, and one of the voices belonged to Valdez, who was probably there with a helper or her buyer, then it really does fit they might have killed her if they found her and realized she had overheard everything that they'd been talking about."

"And not wanting her death to be linked to the Santa House, they moved the body to the woods. That actually makes perfect sense. Except for the drugging. Who drugged her, and why?"

"I don't know. That part does seem odd. I wonder if…" I was interrupted when my phone rang. "I need to get this." I clicked the answer button on my phone. "That was fast," I said to Donovan.

"I found out who your stalker is."

"The woman in the photo I sent you?"

"Yes. I'm afraid the woman you keep seeing is none other than Maria Bonatello."

Okay, I was not expecting that. I felt like I should respond in some way, but I had no idea what to say. I glanced up and noticed Trevor watching me, so I forced myself to pull myself together. "The reception in here is pretty dicey. I'm going to take this outside," I said to Donovan. I then glanced at Trevor. "I'll be right back."

I could feel his gaze on me as I left the building and headed out onto the sidewalk. I supposed I was going to have to come up with some sort of explanation when I went back inside.

"And how exactly is Maria related to the family?" I asked once I found a spot to have the conversation where I wouldn't be overheard.

"She's Vito's sister," Donovan answered.

"So, she's probably the one sending the texts."

"I think so. She isn't a family member who has been on the radar. She was just twelve when her grandfather killed her father. She attended a private boarding school and seemed to have grown up outside of the immediate influence of the family. After her brother got out of prison, he reached out to her. I'm not sure why, after all this time, she decided that you were responsible for her father's death, but I suspect she may not have had access to the details relating to his death until she reconnected with Vito."

"So, what do I do now?"

"I called and spoke to Woody." Donovan had met Woody when he was here at Thanksgiving. "I sent him the photo, and he is going to try to locate her and bring her in for questioning. I also called and spoke to Vito. He swears he had no idea that his sister was even in Oregon, and to be honest, he seemed pretty peeved about the whole thing. He's trying to establish his role in the family, and he told me that he doesn't have time for distractions. He assured me he would handle things and that I shouldn't worry about it."

"Handle things? What does that mean? Is he going to hurt her?"

"I didn't get the feeling he meant her harm. If I had to guess, he will simply call her and demand that she return to New York."

"Do you think she will?"

"I think she will. Maria is only twenty-two. Her father and grandfather are both dead, which puts Vito, as her older brother and a top member of the family, in a position of authority over her. I know that sounds antiquated, but the hierarchy that exists within the family is generally respected."

"So, that's it? I don't need to worry about the texts or the possibility there is someone out there gunning for me?"

"I think the texts were probably a prank, and while I would caution you not to let your guard down, I don't think you are in any imminent danger. I do plan to follow up on things to ensure that Maria does actually return to New York, but I think you can stop looking over your shoulder."

"Good to know."

After I hung up with Donovan, I headed back in to face the questions I knew Trevor would have. I hadn't wanted to worry him, so I hadn't mentioned that my stalker was here in Cutter's Cove, but now that Donovan seemed to have handled things, I supposed I should tell him.

"Sorry about that," I said. "The call kept cutting in and out, but the reception outside was much better."

"Is something up?" he asked.

I decided to answer honestly. "Donovan found out that the texts I've been receiving are from Vito's younger sister, Maria. She is also the woman with the dark hair I've been seeing around town the past couple of days."

"She's here?" he demanded.

"She is, but not to worry. Donovan has things handled. He called and spoke to Vito, who claims he didn't even know she was here. He assured Donovan that he wished me no ill will, and would handle things with his sister."

"Handle things? How?"

"Donovan seems to think Maria will do whatever Vito tells her to do. He also called Woody as a precaution, and Woody is going to try to track her down."

He began placing pepperoni on a pizza. "Are you sure her being here doesn't put you in danger?"

"I guess one can never be sure of something like that," I answered honestly. "But if she really wanted me dead, she's had plenty of opportunities to make that happen. I think she's just angry and upset about what happened to her father and wanted to scare me."

He placed the pie in the oven. "Why now?"

"Donovan thinks it's possible that she didn't even know about my involvement in her father's death until after Vito got out of prison. Not that I was actually responsible for his death, but I suppose I can see how she might come to that conclusion." I slipped onto the stool I'd been sitting on before. "Anyway, it sounds like things are being handled, so I'm not going to worry about it. I have a photo contest to get ready for, which is exactly how I plan to spend my afternoon."

"How are the photos coming along?"

I shrugged. "Okay. I'm still trying to find the one thing that will make my collage stand out, but I think I'm beginning to get some perspective. I have quite a few photos that I think will work, but I'm going to head over to the lot where the carnival is being set up, and then I am going to head over to the park for some additional shots. What time do you think you'll be off?"

"Around four. Will you be home by then?"

"Probably, but text me just in case." I slid off the stool. "Mom is out this evening, so maybe we can grab some food and settle in and watch a movie."

"Sounds good to me. I'll call you."

After I left the restaurant, I headed toward the lot where the carnival folks were setting up the rides and game booths. The carnival was a popular attraction in the area that brought tourists from as far away as Portland. The weather had been dicey lately, but it sounded like the forecast for the weekend was dry and sunny, which I supposed was better for those wanting to partake of the rides and games than the snow we'd been enjoying for the past week or so.

After I took several shots of the crew setting up the rides, I headed toward the community center where I knew Mom and the other volunteers were making candy. The candy they made would be sold over the weekend, and the proceeds would be used for community projects.

"Something smells wonderful," I said after joining the crew in the kitchen.

"We're making the peanut butter fudge," one of the women answered. "The chocolate fudge is cooling if you'd like to try a piece."

"Thanks. I'd love a piece."

I nibbled on the candy while the women chatted about the latest gossip. If there was one thing you could say about the women of Cutter's Cove, it was that if there was something to know, you could pretty well bet that the women who manned the gossip hotline were going to know it.

"So, I understand you are the one who found Holly Quinn's body up on the mountain near Dooley's Farm," a woman I only knew as Edna said.

"Yes. I was up there taking photos for a contest when I stumbled upon her."

"Such a darn shame. I can't imagine why that girl would have been out walking around in a storm with barely a stitch on."

"Young women these days seem to think it's more important to look good than to wear clothing appropriate for the conditions," one of the other women said.

"I heard she'd been at The Rusty Nail earlier in the evening," Edna said.

"I suppose that might explain her clothes, but I don't know why she would be hanging out in a place like that, especially since she was involved in a lawsuit with the owner of the bar," a woman named Rosa huffed, with a tone that made it clear she didn't consider The Rusty Nail to be an appropriate place for a proper young woman.

"I heard that the new owner of the bar sank all his money into the remodel, and would have to close the place down if he lost the lawsuit he was involved in," a woman who had been introduced as Rayleen informed the group. "I heard that a man who's interested in the property wants to tear the place down. No one wants to see The Rusty Nail shut down. It's practically a Cutter's Cove landmark."

I wasn't sure, but this sounded like information Woody might be interested in. "I need to get going," I said to the group. "It's been fun chatting with you, but I have a lot to get done today. Have fun with your candy making, and thanks for the sample; it was really good."

After I left, I called Woody. He didn't answer his phone, so I left a message. I then headed over to The Rusty Nail. It might be early in the day for a drink, but not all that early for someone like me who actually had sleuthing on her mind. I sat down at the bar and ordered a glass of white wine, and then introduced myself to the bartender whose name I already knew was Dave. I opened a dialogue that would get him chatting before I eventually brought things around to my real reason for being there.

"Have you worked here long?" I asked as the man began to wipe down the bar, which I suspected was a nervous habit since the bar had been spotless when I sat down. It was a nice touch, and it did seem to create a homey feel, so maybe the motion was designed to put the customer at ease. There was something about the slow circular motion as he worked his way in one direction and then the other. His hands were rough looking, with visible calluses, which seemed to indicate he must enjoy some sort of physical activity when he wasn't working at the bar. He might chop wood for extra income, perhaps he liked to tinker with old cars, or maybe he was into woodworking.

"I've been here at this bar goin' on thirty years," he answered.

"Thirty years? I thought Rowen Morton just bought this place a few years ago."

He paused and held the rag still. The large ring covered in tiny diamonds on his finger provided an interesting contrast to his work-worn hands. "He did. I used to work for a man named Bill Fitzgerald, but when he retired and sold the bar, I stayed on in spite of the ownership change. Folks come in to see ol' Dave, who always has an open ear and a bit of advice to dole out. Couldn't let them down now, could I?"

"No, I guess not. It sounds like this bar means a lot to you."

"It does. In a way, the bar is like my family. I wanted to buy it myself when Bill sold it, but I couldn't put together the funding. I was happy when Rowen bought it and wanted to keep me on. I'm not sure what I'd do if I didn't have this place to come to each day."

"I guess if you come in every day like you said, you might have been here on Friday."

"I always work the late shift on Friday and Saturday," Dave confirmed. "Those are our busiest times."

"I guess you remember Holly Quinn being here."

"Yeah. I remember seeing her. Nice girl."

"Did you hear that she died?"

His eyes grew wide. "Died? What happened? She seemed fine when she was here. A bit chatty, I suppose, but fine. Was she in another accident?"

I had to admit that his shock at the news seemed legitimate, but it was hard to imagine that a bartender wouldn't have heard the news that seemed to have spread through town like a wildfire. "I'm not sure how she died, but I heard she was drugged. I'm thinking that maybe whoever drugged her must have killed her. What do you think?"

"Can't see why anyone would drug her, and I certainly can't see why anyone would kill her. She was a nice enough girl. She came in here a few times a week, and usually sat right here at the bar and chatted with me. Of course, she wasn't really right after the accident if you know what I mean."

"No. What do you mean?"

"I think the accident she was in messed with her head. She seemed paranoid when she had no reason to be, and sometimes she told me stories that made no sense. I think she might have been losing time."

"Losing time?"

"She'd tell me stories that just couldn't be true based on the timelines she created. I guess that's understandable given the serious nature of what happened to her."

This was the first time I stopped to consider the fact that perhaps the story Holly had told me was less than accurate. Of course, she did die, and someone did dump her body, so it wasn't like she was making the whole thing up.

I took a final sip of my wine and set a twenty-dollar bill on the counter. "It was nice talking to you." I slid off the stool. "Have a happy holiday."

With that, I headed toward Woody's office. He hadn't gotten around to calling me back yet, but the more I thought about it, the more certain I was that we'd both been wrong about what had happened to Holly Quinn.

Chapter 11

When I got to Woody's office, the woman in the reception area gave me the oddest look. I told her I was there to see Woody, and she told me to have a seat. She headed down the hallway, I assumed to let him know I was there, and when she returned, Woody was on her heels.

"Is everything okay?" I asked after noticing the grim expression on his face.

"Come on back to my office. We can talk there."

Oh, I didn't like this at all. Woody was often tired and sometimes even grumpy, but he rarely wore the doomsday expression he wore today.

"What is it?" I asked the minute I sat down. "Did you find out who killed Holly?"

"No. My news is not about Holly."

My stomach sank. "Then what?"

"I found Maria Bonatello."

I smiled. "That's good. Right? We wanted to find her and question her about the texts."

"We can't question her. She's dead."

My smile faded. "Dead? What…" I was about to ask what happened, but suddenly I knew. "Vito."

He nodded. "As far as I know, and as far as Donovan knew when I spoke to him, Vito is in New York, but yeah, Donovan thinks Vito is behind the seemingly random shooting in the park."

I placed my hand on my stomach. I was pretty sure I was going to be sick. "I need to call him. Donovan. I need to find out what he knows."

"He's on his way here, and in the air, so I doubt you'll be able to reach him. He wanted to tell you what happened himself, but you didn't answer when he called."

I looked at my phone. There were three missed calls from Donovan. I supposed I really should turn on my ringer.

I swallowed hard. "This is my fault. Maria died because I noticed her following me and Donovan spoke to Vito on my behalf."

"It isn't your fault. You couldn't have known what would happen, and even if you could predict what might happen, she was the one threatening you, not the other way around. You can't blame yourself for what happened to Maria."

I lifted a brow as a tear slid down my cheek. "Can't I? The minute Donovan told me that Vito would handle Maria, I knew deep inside what was going to happen. Vito's grandfather killed his father and his uncle when they came after me, and now Vito has killed his sister for doing the same thing. I know I shouldn't feel bad. And to be honest, I didn't feel bad when Mario and Clay were killed since I knew they really did want me dead. But Maria? I'm not sure she was even a danger to me. I think she heard about my role in her father's death and decided that I needed to pay some sort of price for my part in the whole thing. I know she threatened me, but I really do think her threats were just that, threats. She had a lot of opportunities to kill me if she really wanted me dead."

Woody placed his hand over mine. "That may be true, but you didn't do anything wrong. If you stop to think about it, all you did was to ask Donovan if he recognized the woman in the photo. She'd been following you. Wondering about her was a natural thing to do."

I knew Woody was right. I knew that Maria's death was on Vito and not on me. I didn't understand how a man could kill his sister, but I remembered the comment Donovan made about the obedience that was required within the family to those who came above you in the hierarchy. Vito probably told Maria to stop following me and come home. She probably declined to do one or both, so he had her killed. He was the leader of the family now, and due to the fact he was new to the role, I supposed disobedience from anyone could not be tolerated. Allowing his sister to defy him would have been a show of weakness. Still, how could he do this?

"Thanks for letting me know what happened," I said. "I guess I know in my mind that I'm not responsible for what happened, but in my heart, I am going to mourn for the girl who never really had a chance."

"She had a chance. It sounds like she was out of the family and everything that came with being part of the family, but she willingly stepped back in. She must have known that going off on her own the way she did could only lead to trouble."

I understood what Woody was saying, but it didn't make things easier to accept. I needed time to process everything that had happened. I texted Trevor and told him that I was heading home, and if he still wanted to spend time together, he could meet me there.

Chapter 12

By the time Saturday rolled around, Mac had come home, Donovan had arrived and planned to stay through Christmas, Maria's body had been sent to her family in New York, and life had settled back into a somewhat normal routine. I'd turned in my collage of photos to the magazine running the contest, and while I hadn't heard back yet, I felt really good about the final product I'd come up with. I supposed the one dark cloud in my life was the fact that Holly's killer hadn't been caught. The official cause of death, as declared by the medical examiner was heart failure, but the ME also said that the drug found in her system should have lowered her inhibitions, but should not have caused her heart to fail. Her body had been found out in the storm, so the ME concluded it was the bracing cold, combined with the drugs that led to her death.

Of course, I had reason to believe she died in the Santa House and had been moved into the storm after her death, but I had no evidence to support that theory other than my discussion with a ghost, so I kept my opinion to myself. The reality was, if not for the fact I had chatted with Holly before she moved on, the theory that she'd simply gotten wasted, wandered into the storm, and died, would have been one I considered to be a good one.

Woody admitted the explanation the ME came up with was most likely the one he would have gone with as well if he didn't know better.

The question was: if Holly hadn't wandered into the storm and died, and the drugs in her system weren't the sort to stop her heart, how had she died?

And then there was the Santa House supervisor, and the illegal smuggling operation Woody and I were convinced was going on right beneath our noses. The theory was a good one, but the problem was that while the theory seemed solid, we really had no proof. Ms. Valdez had certainly covered her tracks, and she seemed to be ready with both an invoice and an explanation for all the merchandise moved into and out of the building. Woody had shared his frustration with the situation. If Jessica Valdez had come to the Santa House with a helper or her buyer on the night Holly died and found her hiding in the dressing room, I supposed it tracked that she might have killed Holly to protect her secret. Sure, the medical examiner had stated that the use of death was heart failure, but that didn't mean that the heart failure wasn't helped along by a pillow held to her face, or an injection into her veins.

However she died, Woody and I figured that once Holly was dead, Ms. Valdez would have had the motive to move the body to avoid any association with the Santa House, which would have brought about a lot of attention she wouldn't have wanted. Of course, she may have found Holly already dead and moved the body for the same reason. Holly had said she'd heard voices and had run and hidden, but she didn't remember anything after that. Could the extra adrenalin produced from her fear have been the catalyst that caused her heart to stop?

And then there was the question of who drugged Holly. Since it appeared she was drugged at the bar, we assumed that it was the bar owner who was also a defendant in her lawsuit who'd drugged her, but to what end? Had he known the drugs would lead to heart failure? Or was he simply trying to mess with her as some sort of a threat to back off the lawsuit?

Woody and I had gone around and around on this. Our current theory was that Rowen Morton, the bar owner, had slipped Holly the drugs and then drove her to the Santa House. We didn't know his motive for drugging her, but it appeared Holly had fallen asleep and hadn't died until Jessica Valdez and a helper or her buyer came in, scaring the girl and sending her running. When Valdez found Jessica dead in the dressing room, she'd panicked and moved the body.

Based on the evidence we'd gathered, we'd come up with a good theory, but as I'd said in the beginning, we didn't have a lick of proof to support any of it.

Trevor and I had a shift at the Santa House today, and I was looking forward to playing an elf to his Santa. When we'd played those roles as teenagers, we'd brought Tucker along to play the part of Tucker, the Red-Nosed Reindeer. I'd asked the event coordinator if he could come along this year as well, and she'd approved my request, so it was the three of us who headed into town.

"It looks like the line wraps around the building," Trevor said as we approached the Santa House. The attraction didn't even open for another half hour, so I couldn't imagine what the line was going to look like by then.

"I guess we should be prepared for a long day. I hope they have enough candy canes. I heard that they ran out one day last week, and the poor volunteers ended up with teary-eyed children and angry parents."

"Let's check the supply when we get there," Trevor suggested. "If it looks like we're going to be short, we can call Mac and have her bring us some more."

Once we parked and let ourselves into the Santa House, Trevor and I changed into our costumes. Tucker's costume consisted of a pair of reindeer antlers, which we decided to wait to put on until we were ready to open the door. The woman in charge of running the gift shop for today showed up shortly after we did, and the girl who was in charge of the photos showed up shortly after that.

"It looks like half the town has come out today," the woman who was going to be running the gift shop said after looking out the window as we prepared to open. "Which is crazy since we've actually been busy all week."

"Of course, we were closed for a couple of days while the police did their investigation," the girl doing the photos, whose nametag read Polly, pointed out.

"Did you know Holly?" I asked.

"Sure. She was a regular volunteer. In fact, she was probably here more often than any of the other elves."

"It's a shame what happened to her," the woman who ran the gift shop said.

"I heard she got wasted and wandered into a storm, but that doesn't feel right to me," Polly said. "Sure, Holly liked to go out and have a drink now and again, but she told me she had a heart problem, so she drank responsibly and never did drugs."

"A heart problem?" I asked.

She nodded. "Some sort of a murmur. She didn't go into the specifics, but I remember her saying that she needed to avoid anything that might alter her natural rhythm. She avoided caffeine, as well."

I glanced at Trevor. He raised a brow. Had we just figured out why Holly had died? "I need to make a call," I said. "I won't be long." I grabbed my phone and found a quiet place to call Woody. I shared what I'd heard about Holly's heart condition with him, and he said he'd look into it.

By the time I returned to the main room, it was time to open the doors. The next six hours flew by as a constant line of children of all ages filed through. I was really hoping the crew who was supposed to relieve us at four would be on time since, I for one, was exhausted by the time the clock reached the three o'clock hour.

"Hello, and what is your name?" I asked the blond-haired girl with the long pigtails who had moved to the front of the line.

"Sophie."

"I'm going to lift you onto Santa's lap if that is okay." I'd learned not to pick up a child without asking first.

"I don't want to talk to Santa. I want to talk to the reindeer."

I glanced at Tucker, who had been such a good sport, but I could see was tiring as well. "Is it okay if Sophie whispers her secret to you?"

He lifted his head and thumped his tail.

Sophie approached cautiously. She got down on the floor next to Tucker, leaned in close, and whispered to him. She then hugged him around the neck, kissed the top of his head, and stood up.

"Before you go, do you want to tell Santa what you want for Christmas?" I asked.

"The reindeer knows. He can tell Santa."

I glanced at the woman who stood nearby, and who I assumed was the girl's mother. She had a look of desperation in her eyes.

"Maybe you should whisper it to me as well. Tucker, the Reindeer, is getting old, and he doesn't always remember things like he should."

The girl looked hesitant but eventually nodded. I got down on the floor, so I was closer to her height. She whispered in my ear that she wanted Santa to bring her daddy home. I was sure there was a story there, but it wasn't my business, so I hugged her and told her I'd pass along the message. The girl's mom sent the child to get a candy cane while I whispered Sophie's wish in her mother's ear.

"I was afraid of that. Sophie's father is in the Army. He's overseas and won't make it home this year."

“Maybe you can set up a call or something,” I suggested.

“Perhaps. I’ll see what I can do.”

While most of the kids wished for toys and games, it was the wishes like Sophie’s that tugged at my heartstrings. I was heading back to my spot by Santa’s side when I noticed something under his chair. The sun was coming through the window at an angle as it set, causing a reflection that I hadn’t noticed before. I bent down to see what it was that had slipped under the chair. Whatever it was had rolled all the way to the center, so I decided to wait until Santa got up, and we could move the chair. I knew that the Santa chair would be roped off during the shift change, so I could retrieve the object then.

As I hoped they would, our relief shift showed up right at four, so we drug the rope across the entrance to the Santa chair, and announced that Santa would be taking a twenty-minute break, but would be back shortly.

“There’s something under the chair,” I said to Trevor. “I noticed it earlier, but it’s all the way toward the middle, so I decided to wait for the break. I think you’ll need to lift the front of the chair while I get down on the floor and grab it.”

The chair was a huge overstuffed type chair that weighed as much as a small sofa. Trevor lifted the front, and I laid down on the hardwood floor and reached forward. I slid the small stone toward me. Trevor lowered the chair, and then we both headed toward the changing room.

“I think I might know who killed, or at least who moved, Holly.”

Chapter 13

I called Woody with the news that I'd found a small diamond under the Santa chair, and that I'd also noticed that Dave, the bartender, had a diamond missing from the ring he wore. Sure, he could have lost the diamond at any point, and I imagined if asked about it, he'd tell a tale of it having gone missing long ago, but what were the odds that the man who had served her the drink she'd enjoyed just prior to becoming dizzy, wasn't the one who added the drugs that eventually killed her.

Of course, that didn't explain why Dave had been in the Santa House unless he'd been the second person in the pair who'd shown up later in the evening. If Dave was working with Jessica, that would explain why he was there, and it might even explain how Jessica could have managed to move her, but it really didn't explain why he'd drugged her. I felt like our theory had a big gap that needed something to fill it.

"Okay, so Holly goes to the bar after her shift at the Santa House," I said to Woody and Trevor, who were sitting at the same conference table I sat at in Woody's office. "She has high heels on, so Owen gives her a ride. He drops her off, and she has drinks with her realtor. At some point, the realtor gets a call and leaves. I assume she was still feeling fine at this point."

"I spoke to Chris, and he said that Holly seemed fine, and at no time while he was with her did she complain about feeling ill," Woody confirmed.

I glanced at Tucker, who was snoring softly at my feet. The poor puppy was exhausted after playing a reindeer for half the day. "Okay, so she must have been drugged after Chris left," I concluded. "The fact that she didn't complain about not feeling well until well after he left supports this as well."

"I can see where it might be logical that Dave is the one who drugged her, but why? What was his end game?" Trevor asked.

"He did seem to care a lot about the bar, and the lawsuit had put the bar owner in a position where he might have to sell. Maybe Dave was trying to save the bar," I suggested.

"Okay, then how was drugging Holly going to save the bar, unless Dave knew she had a heart condition and planned to kill her?" Trevor asked. "That seems pretty risky. Even if he knew about her heart condition, there is no way he would actually know that she would die."

"And the idea that he was partnered up with Ms. Valdez isn't really working for me either," Woody said.

"Yet, it does seem that we have circumstantial evidence to suggest that he was in the Santa House at some point. I suppose we could match the diamond I found to the ring to further confirm that," I suggested.

"I feel like a lot is going on, but none of it fits," Trevor said. "Holly went to the bar on the night she died. She ended up with drugs in her system, which eventually stopped her heart, and we assume she ingested the drugs at the bar since she remembers that she began to feel dizzy while she was there."

"And the cocktail waitress said she told her that she wasn't feeling well," I added.

"The bar owner brings her to the Santa House so she can get her phone," Trevor continued. "It sounded like he dropped her off and left."

"She came in and sat down in the chair. She fell asleep. At some point, she heard voices and someone at the door, so and ran and hid. That's all she remembered until the cleaning lady came in. She tried to talk to her, but was already dead," I added.

"Which means it has to be the people who came in and caused her to run to the dressing room who moved her body," Trevor concluded.

"Unless she was already dead before she heard the voices at the door," I said.

Trevor raised a brow.

"Holly told us she was asleep in the Santa chair when she heard the voices that caused her to run and hide. We assumed she was alive at that point, but what if she wasn't? What if she had already died and her body had already been moved, and it was her ghost that had been asleep in the chair? What if she ran and hid when she heard voices, but since she was already dead, she wasn't actually there to find?"

"So, she died, and someone moved her before she heard the voices?" Woody asked.

"Perhaps," I nodded. "And if that is true, then perhaps the voices she remembers hearing actually belonged to the cleaning lady. She said that she heard voices and ran and hid, and the next thing she remembered was the cleaning lady and trying to talk to her, so what if this all happened a lot closer together than it sounded at first?"

"That does make sense," Woody said, "but if that is what happened, who killed her, or at least who moved her?"

"My money is on a joint effort between the bar owner and the bartender," I said. "We can conclude that Dave was at the Santa House at some point due to the presence of the diamond under the chair. And Holly told us the bar owner dropped her off there, but why would he just drop her off at an empty building if she was dizzy?"

"He wouldn't unless he knew she would pass out and planned to come back for some reason," Trevor said.

"Exactly." I paused and rolled the idea around in my mind. "It makes sense to me that Dave slipped the drug into Holly's drink, and when she began to feel dizzy and wanted to leave, Rowen gave her a ride. He dropped her off at the Santa House, knowing she'd pass out at any moment and planned to come back with Dave after the bar closed and do whatever it was they planned to do. When they arrived, they found her dead in the Santa chair, so they panicked and drove her up to the top of the jeep trail where they dumped her body."

"That all makes sense," Woody said. "But how did they get in?"

"Maybe he rigged the door so he could get back in," I suggested.

"So, how does Ms. Valdez fit into this?" Trevor asked.

"Maybe she doesn't," I said. "Maybe she was never even there. If Holly was already dead when she heard the voices at the door, it could very well have been the cleaning lady. She might have brought a helper, or maybe she was talking on the phone, which is why she fumbled the code."

"So, are we saying that Ms. Valdez isn't involved in illegal activity?" Trevor asked.

"I don't know," Woody answered. "I still suspect that something is going on, but so far, she's been able to provide invoices and an explanation for everything. Maybe she really isn't doing anything wrong in spite of the nagging feeling I have in my gut that tells me she is."

"Okay, so how do we prove our theory?" I asked.

"We play Dave and Rowen against each other," Woody suggested. "I'll pick them both up, offer both a deal and make sure they know that whoever talks first, will get a slightly lesser sentence than whoever holds out."

Chapter 14

"Who bogarted all the green ribbon?" Mac demanded as Cooper nipped at her feet.

"There was a whole spool a minute ago." I looked around the table where Mac, Trevor, and I were wrapping gifts for the disadvantaged children's toy drive. "Maybe it rolled onto the floor." I bent over to look, but the floor, unlike the table, chairs, and countertop, was clear of ribbons, boxes, and wrapping paper. "Just use the red ribbon. I'd go and look for more green, but we're almost done."

"Finally," Mac groaned as she bent over and picked up the puppy I had definitely decided to keep. "When you said you were going to pick up a few toys for the toy drive and needed help wrapping, I figured you'd have a bag or two full of goodies, not a truckload."

I shrugged. "What can I say? I am an impulse buyer. Always have been. Did you remember to label all the packages with boy or girl and the appropriate age? I'm going to take them and drop them off once we are done here."

"I did," Mac confirmed.

I glanced at Trevor. "Mine are all wrapped and labeled. I'm going to take a short break and call into work to make sure everything is going smoothly."

"And I'm going to go up and get ready for my date," Mac seconded.

"Since you're going to *The Nutcracker* in Portland, will you be staying at Ty's tonight?" I said.

"That's the plan, but I will be home tomorrow afternoon. I have some work I want to finish up before Christmas. Ty is going to drive me back and then just stay through New Year's if that's okay."

"Of course, it's okay. This is your house too."

"That isn't technically correct," Mac pointed out, "but I appreciate the sentiment."

"Mom and Donovan should be back from Seattle tomorrow night, so everyone will be here for Christmas week." I glanced at Trevor. "You should bring a bag. You can sleep on the sofa bed in the attic. That way, you won't have to go back and forth to your place and won't have to worry about driving. I think more snow is in the forecast."

"I might just do that, but tonight I'm cooking, and you are coming to my house with me."

I smiled. "Sounds perfect."

Mac tore off a piece of tape and secured the red ribbon she'd settled on. "By the way, did you figure out what happened to Holly?"

"We did," I answered. "Or at least Woody did. His plan to play the two men against each other worked out perfectly. Dave finally caved and admitted that he put the drugs in Holly's drink. The plan had been to get her wasted, and then take incriminating photos of her that they could use to blackmail her into dropping the lawsuit. Dave planned to put the drugs in her after-dinner drink, which would have worked out in terms of a timeline since the bar would have been closing about the same time she was ready to leave, but then Chris had to leave early, and Holly announced she was going to leave as well, so Dave panicked and gave her the drugs early. When she got dizzy, Rowen offered her a ride. He dropped her at the Santa House. He said she passed out in the Santa chair before he even left. He jimmied the door, so he could get back in, and once the bar closed, Dave and Rowen went back with a camera, but she was already dead. They panicked and moved the body."

"And the Santa House supervisor?" Mac asked. "Was she dealing in illegal goods?"

"Woody doesn't know. He has a hunch she was, but he never found any proof, so that might be a dead-end at this point. After Trevor, Woody, and I discussed that it might have been the cleaning lady who Holly heard on the night she died, Woody spoke to her again, and she did say that she'd been on the phone when she arrived and that had caused her to mess up the keypad. We suspect that by the time she showed up, Holly was already a ghost, but just didn't know it. At first, it seemed like there was a time lag between Holly hearing someone at the door and seeing the cleaning lady, but time seems to work differently in the between world."

Mac stood up. "Well, I'm glad everything was worked out. I'm heading up to make myself irresistible. If you're already gone by the time I come down, I'll see you tomorrow."

After Mac went upstairs, Trevor helped me to load his truck. We took the wrapped packages to the community center and dropped them off. Trevor and I discussed what to do next, but eventually decided to just head to his place, so he could begin the prep work on the dinner he had planned. Neither Mom nor Mac would be home this evening, so I didn't want to be too late. Someone needed to be there to let the dogs out.

"I could just take the food to your house and cook it there since no one will be there," Trevor suggested. "I really want to bring Mac's desk over and set it up while she's out. It will be a surprise when she returns tomorrow."

"That might be a good idea," I answered. "I hate to leave the dogs too long. If you want to bring a bag, you can just stay tonight."

Trevor hesitated. "Really? Are you sure? It will just be the two of us and well..." he let the thought hang.

I crossed the room and put my arms around Trevor's neck. I stood on my tiptoes and kissed him gently on the lips. "I'm sure it's time to take a chance and see where our relationship might take us. I've given this a lot of thought, and I think I'm ready for whatever comes next if you are."

Trevor tightened his arms around me. He didn't reply, but based on the way his lips captured mine, I was willing to bet that he was as ready to move our relationship forward as I was.